D0938512

Nola's Worlds #3

even for a dreamer like me

A BiG THank YOU TO MY LiTTLE BanD OF DREAMERS, ALiCia, GaëL, anD Anna. As alWaYS, a HUGE acKnOWLEDGEMENT TO MY TRaVELiNG COMPaNiONS, KiM anD MÉLaNiE. THE jOURNEY iSN'T OVER YET; HaPPiLY, WE'LL SOON SET OFF aGaiN FOR THE LanD OF NOLa BanaNa. anD FiNaLLY, THank YOU TO aLL OUR READERS FOR THEiR ENTHUSiaSTiC RESPONSES, aS WELL aS TO THOSE WHO'VE HaD CONFiDENCE iN US anD HELPED US WiTH THiS PROjECT.

THank YOU TO
MYLèNE HENRY
NiCOLAS PLaMONDON
CÉCiLia RaViX-ANTONiNi

TO MY PÉPÉ ♡

THank YOU TO CHKLE, JOanY D. LEBLanC, KiRa, anD CaLaMiTY, WHO HELPED SO MUCH WiTH THE COLORiNG. THank YOU TO GaTE anD MY FaMiLY, WHO HaVE SUPPORTED ME iN EVERY SENSE OF THE WORD FROM THE BEGiNNiNG, jUST LikE KiM anD MaTHiEU. ^ ^ anD THank YOU TO EVERYONE WHO PaTiENTLY aWaiTED THE RELEASE OF THiS THiRD VOLUME iN THE ADVENTURES OF NOLa. À BiENTÔT UNTiL THE NEXT THank YOUS. :P

STORY BY MaTHiEU MaRiOLLE
ART BY MiNiKiM
COLORS BY POP
TRanSLaTiON BY ERiCa OLSON JEFFREY anD CaROL KLiO BURRELL

First American edition published in 2010 by Graphic Universe™.
Published by arrangement with MEDIATOON LICENSING — France.

Alta Donna 3 – Même pour une rêveuse comme moi …
© DARGAUD BENELUX (DARGAUD-LOMBARD S.A.) 2009, by Mariolle, MiniKim, Pop.
www.dargaud.com

English translation copyright © 2010 by Lerner Publishing Group, Inc.

Graphic Universe™
A division of Lerner Publishing Group, Inc.
241 First Avenue North
Minneapolis, MN 55401 U.S.A.

Website address: www.lernerbooks.com

The image in this book is used with the permission of:
© iStockphoto.com/Lobke Peers, p. 30.

Library of Congress Cataloging-in-Publication Data

Mariolle, Mathieu.
    Even for a dreamer like me / by Mathieu Mariolle ; illustrated by MiniKim ; colored by Pop. — 1st American ed.
      p. cm. — (Nola's worlds ; #3)
    Summary: Nola learns that the city of Alta Donna is more important than she imagined, and that her storytelling ability is the key to saving her world, the world of stories, and her friends Damiano and Inés.
    ISBN: 978-0-7613-6505-1 (lib. bdg : alk. paper)
    1. Graphic novels. [1. Graphic novels. 2. Imagination—Fiction. 3. Characters in literature—Fiction. 4. Supernatural—Fiction. 5. Ferrets—Fiction.] I. MiniKim, ill. II. Pop, 1978– ill. III. Title.
PZ7.7.M34Eve 2010
741.5'944—dc22
                        2010015215

Manufactured in the United States of America
1 – DP – 7/15/10

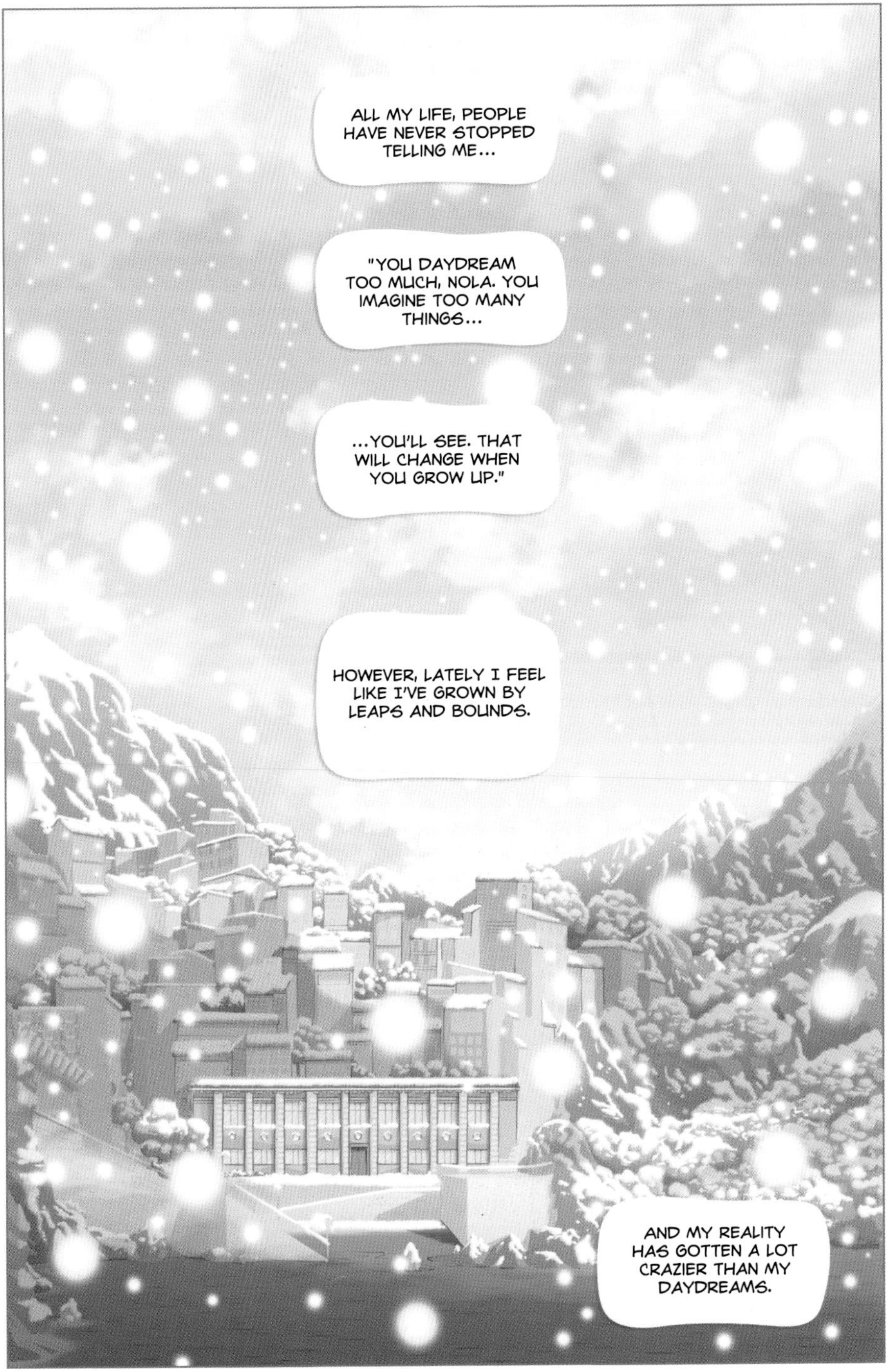
ALL MY LIFE, PEOPLE HAVE NEVER STOPPED TELLING ME...
"YOU DAYDREAM TOO MUCH, NOLA. YOU IMAGINE TOO MANY THINGS...
...YOU'LL SEE. THAT WILL CHANGE WHEN YOU GROW UP."
HOWEVER, LATELY I FEEL LIKE I'VE GROWN BY LEAPS AND BOUNDS.
AND MY REALITY HAS GOTTEN A LOT CRAZIER THAN MY DAYDREAMS.

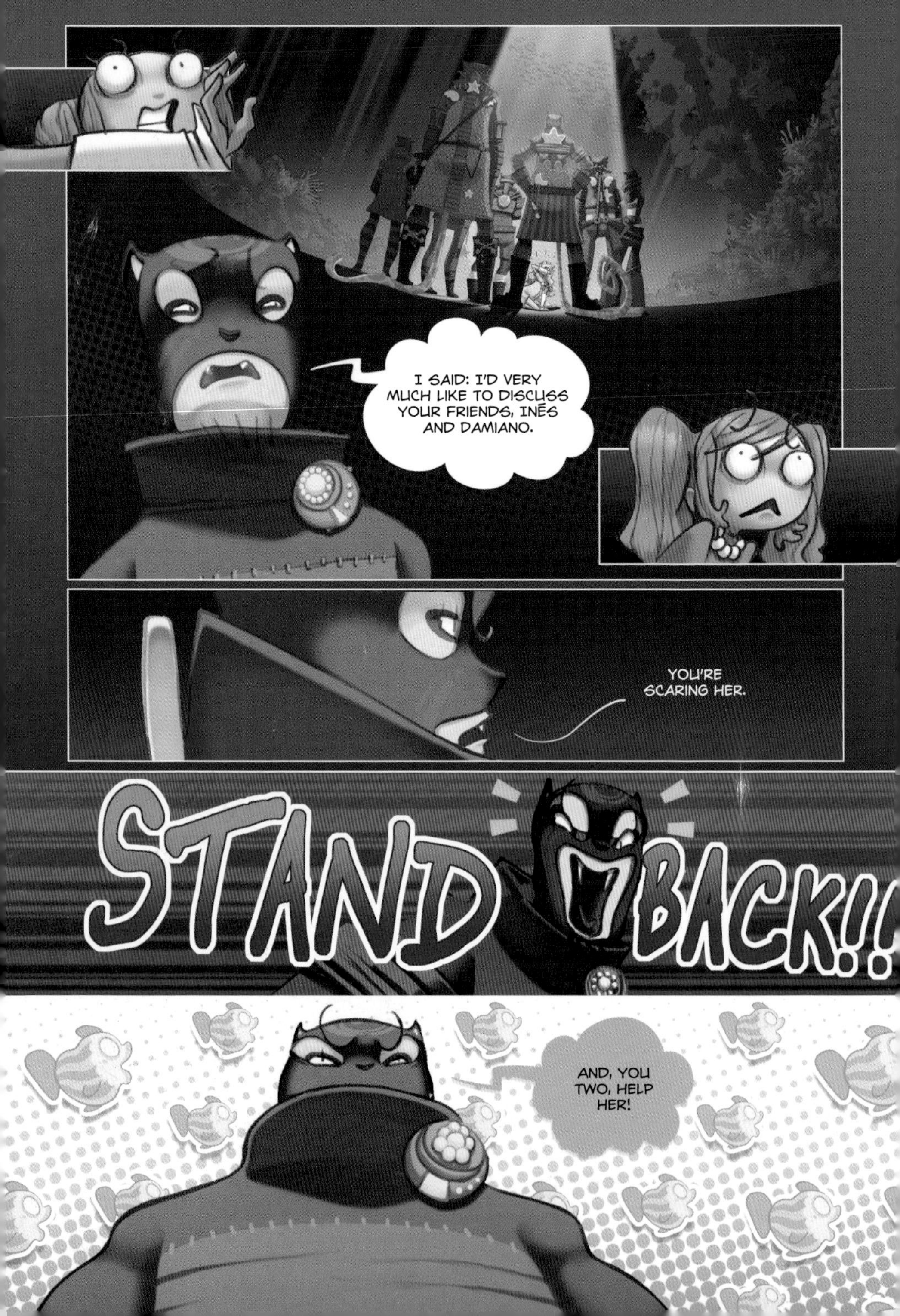
I SAID: I'D VERY MUCH LIKE TO DISCUSS YOUR FRIENDS, INÉS AND DAMIANO.
YOU'RE SCARING HER.
STAND BACK!!
AND, YOU TWO, HELP HER!

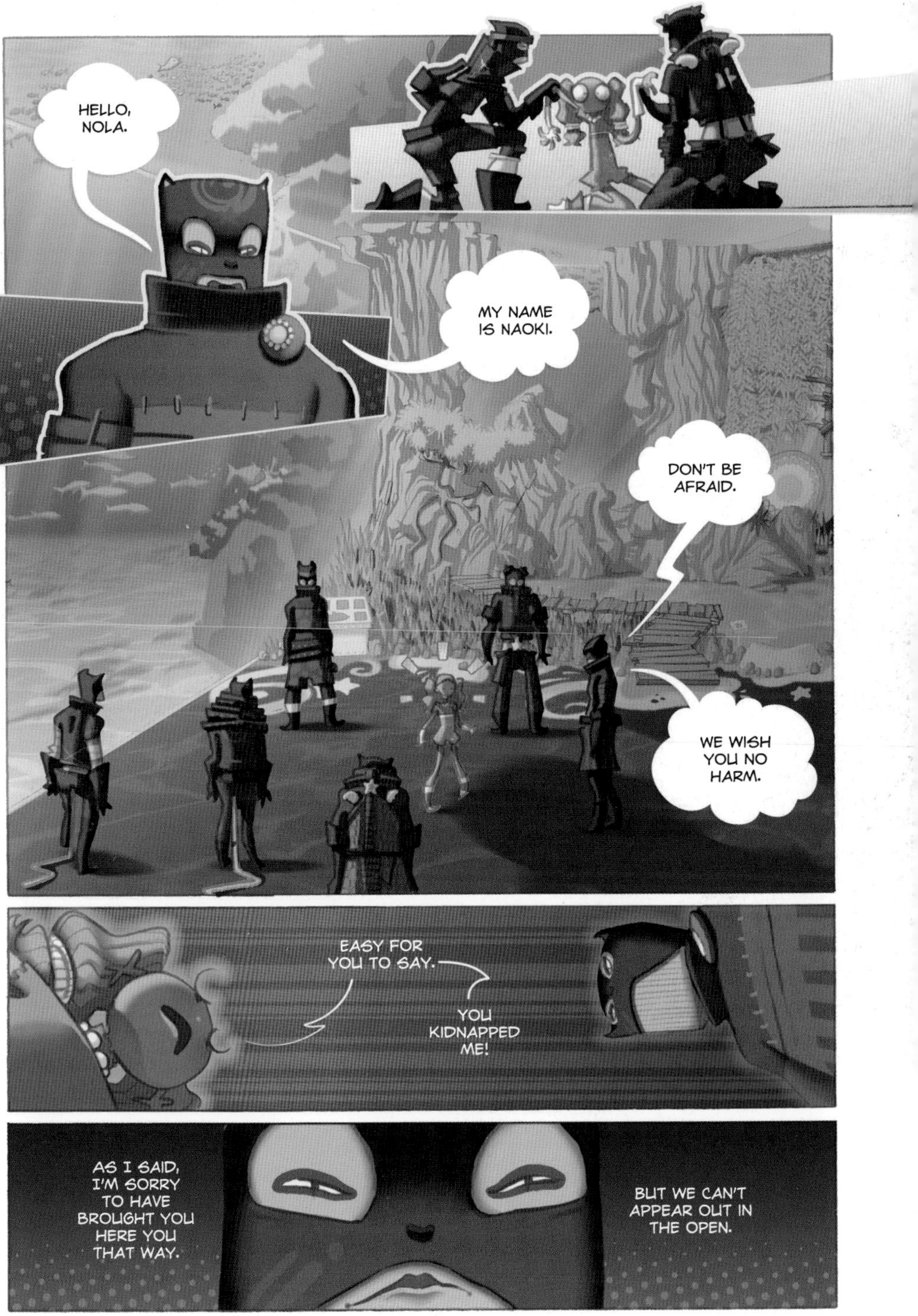
HELLO, NOLA.
MY NAME IS NAOKI.
DON'T BE AFRAID.
WE WISH YOU NO HARM.
EASY FOR YOU TO SAY.
YOU KIDNAPPED ME!
AS I SAID, I'M SORRY TO HAVE BROUGHT YOU HERE YOU THAT WAY.
BUT WE CAN'T APPEAR OUT IN THE OPEN.

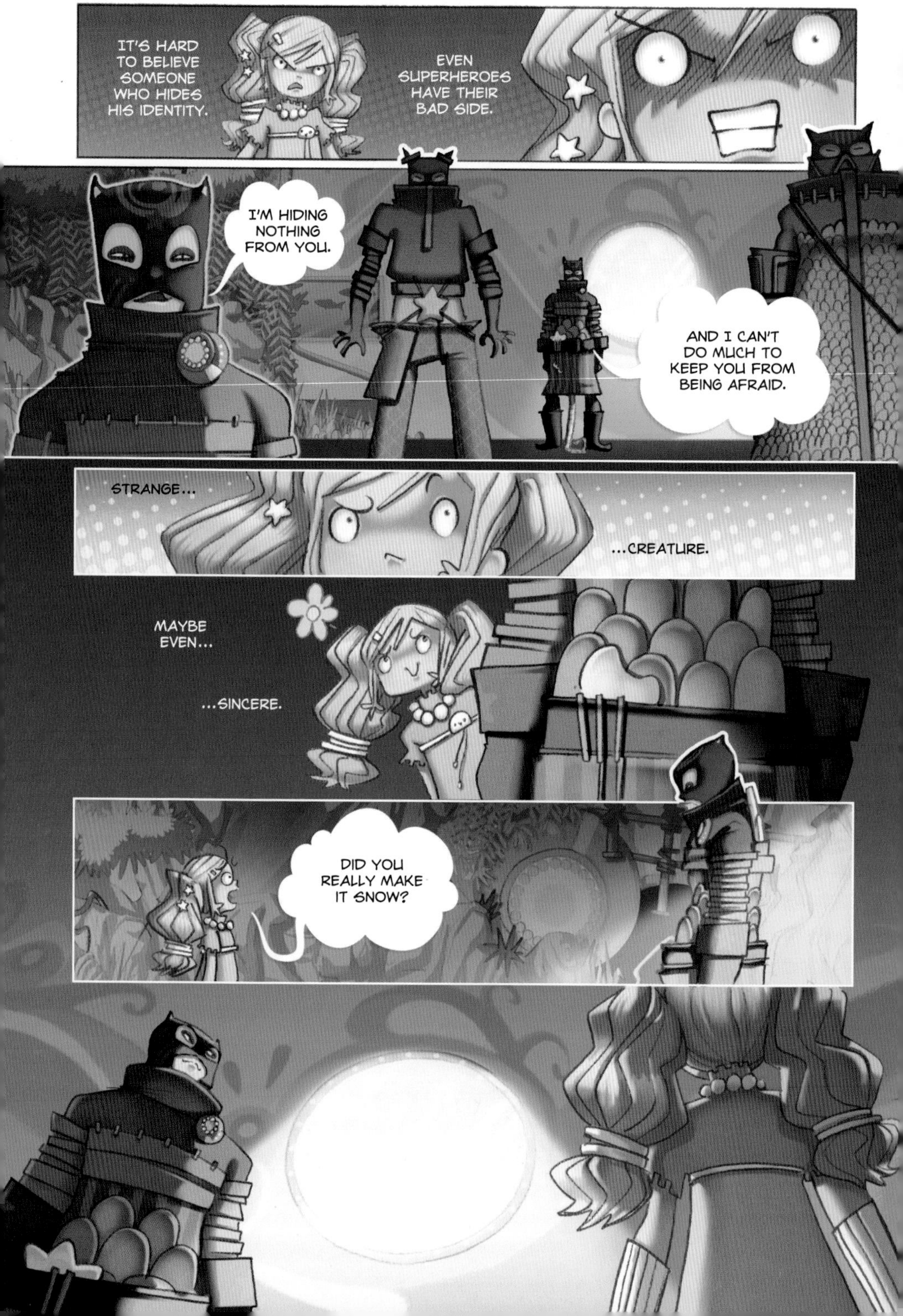
IT'S HARD TO BELIEVE SOMEONE WHO HIDES HIS IDENTITY.
EVEN SUPERHEROES HAVE THEIR BAD SIDE.
I'M HIDING NOTHING FROM YOU.
AND I CAN'T DO MUCH TO KEEP YOU FROM BEING AFRAID.
STRANGE...
...CREATURE.
MAYBE EVEN...
...SINCERE.
DID YOU REALLY MAKE IT SNOW?

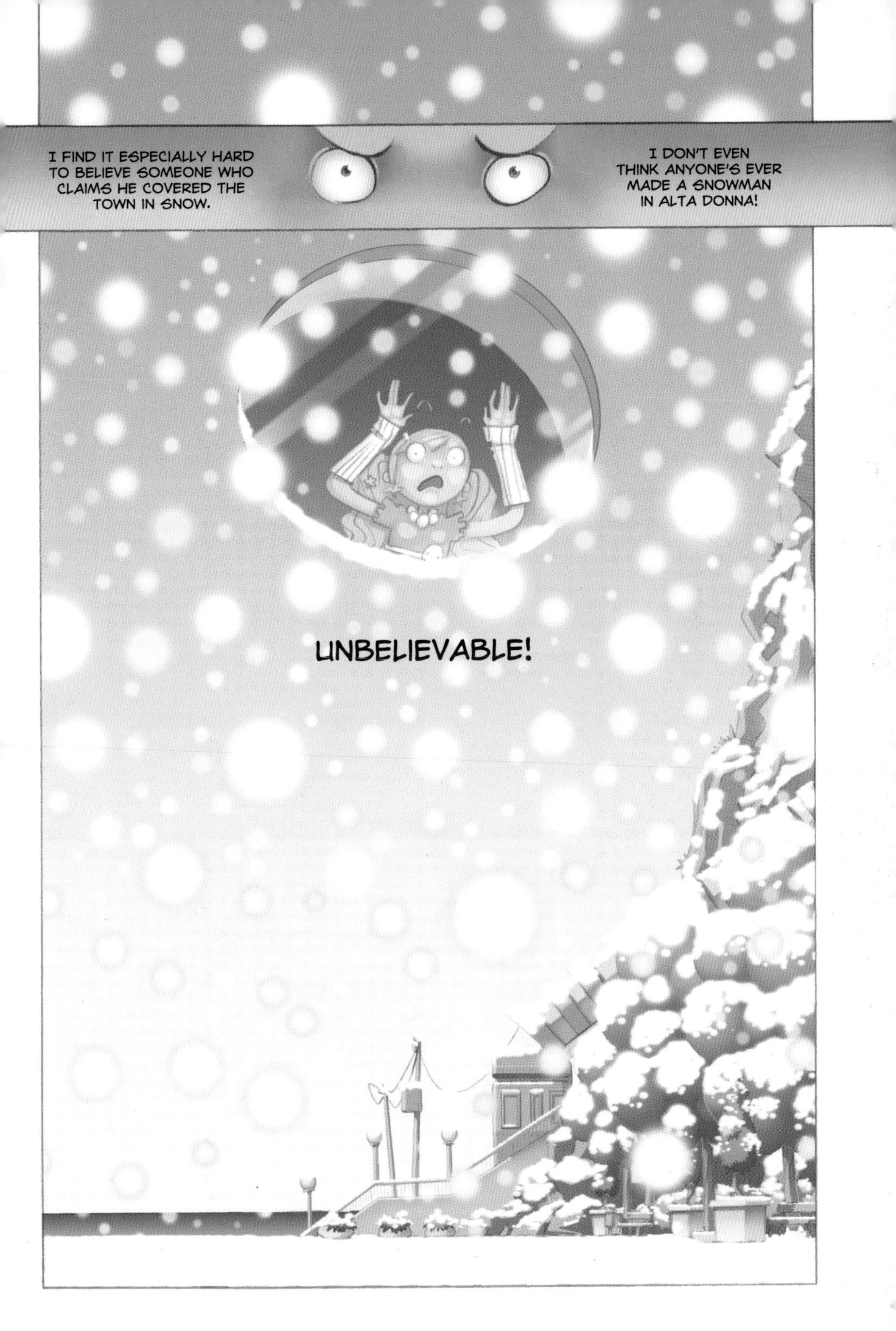
I FIND IT ESPECIALLY HARD TO BELIEVE SOMEONE WHO CLAIMS HE COVERED THE TOWN IN SNOW.
I DON'T EVEN THINK ANYONE'S EVER MADE A SNOWMAN IN ALTA DONNA!
UNBELIEVABLE!

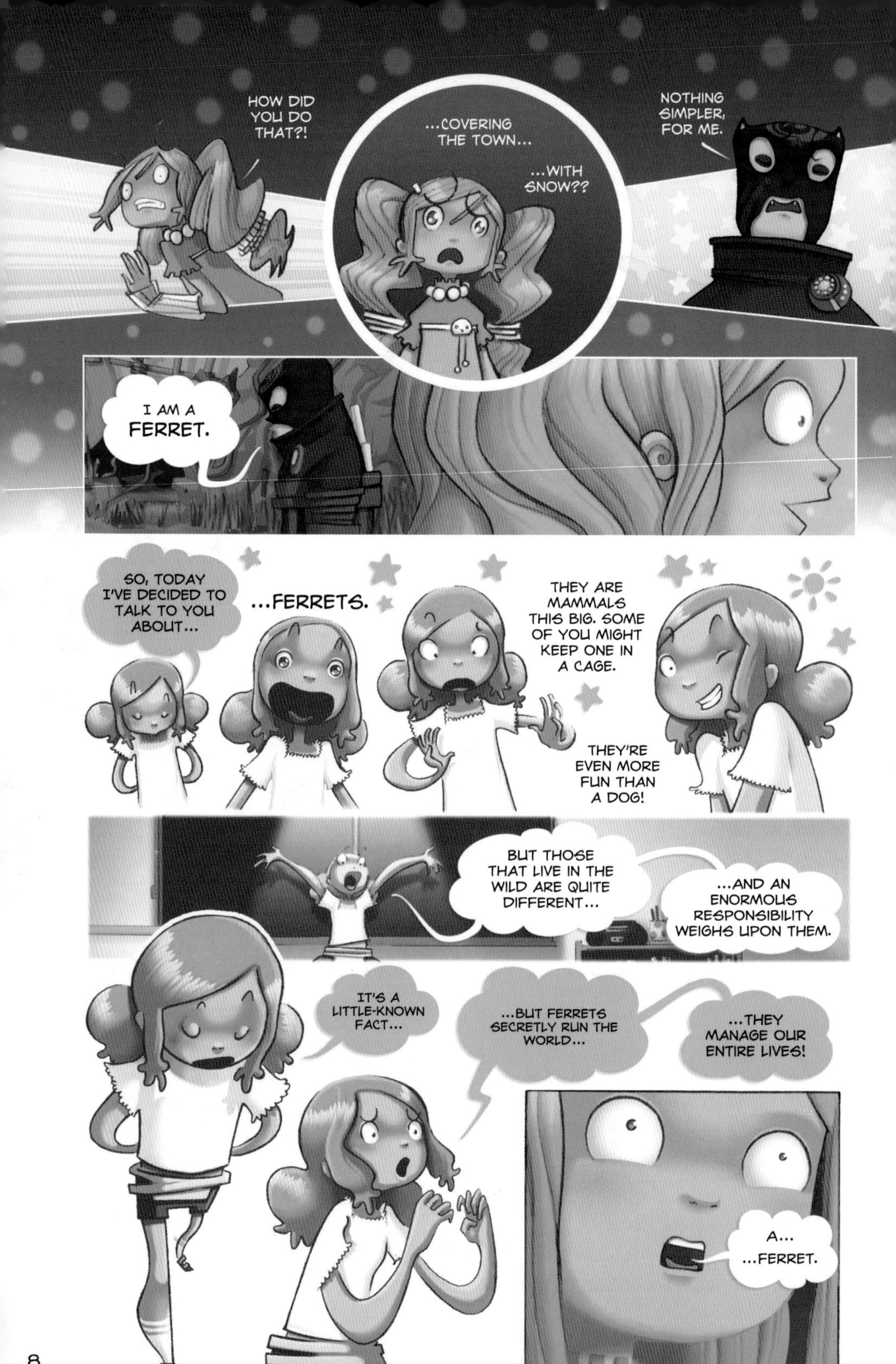
HOW DID YOU DO THAT?!
...COVERING THE TOWN...
...WITH SNOW??
NOTHING SIMPLER, FOR ME.
I AM A FERRET.
SO, TODAY I'VE DECIDED TO TALK TO YOU ABOUT...
...FERRETS.
THEY ARE MAMMALS THIS BIG. SOME OF YOU MIGHT KEEP ONE IN A CAGE.
THEY'RE EVEN MORE FUN THAN A DOG!
BUT THOSE THAT LIVE IN THE WILD ARE QUITE DIFFERENT...
...AND AN ENORMOUS RESPONSIBILITY WEIGHS UPON THEM.
IT'S A LITTLE-KNOWN FACT...
...BUT FERRETS SECRETLY RUN THE WORLD...
...THEY MANAGE OUR ENTIRE LIVES!
A...
...FERRET.

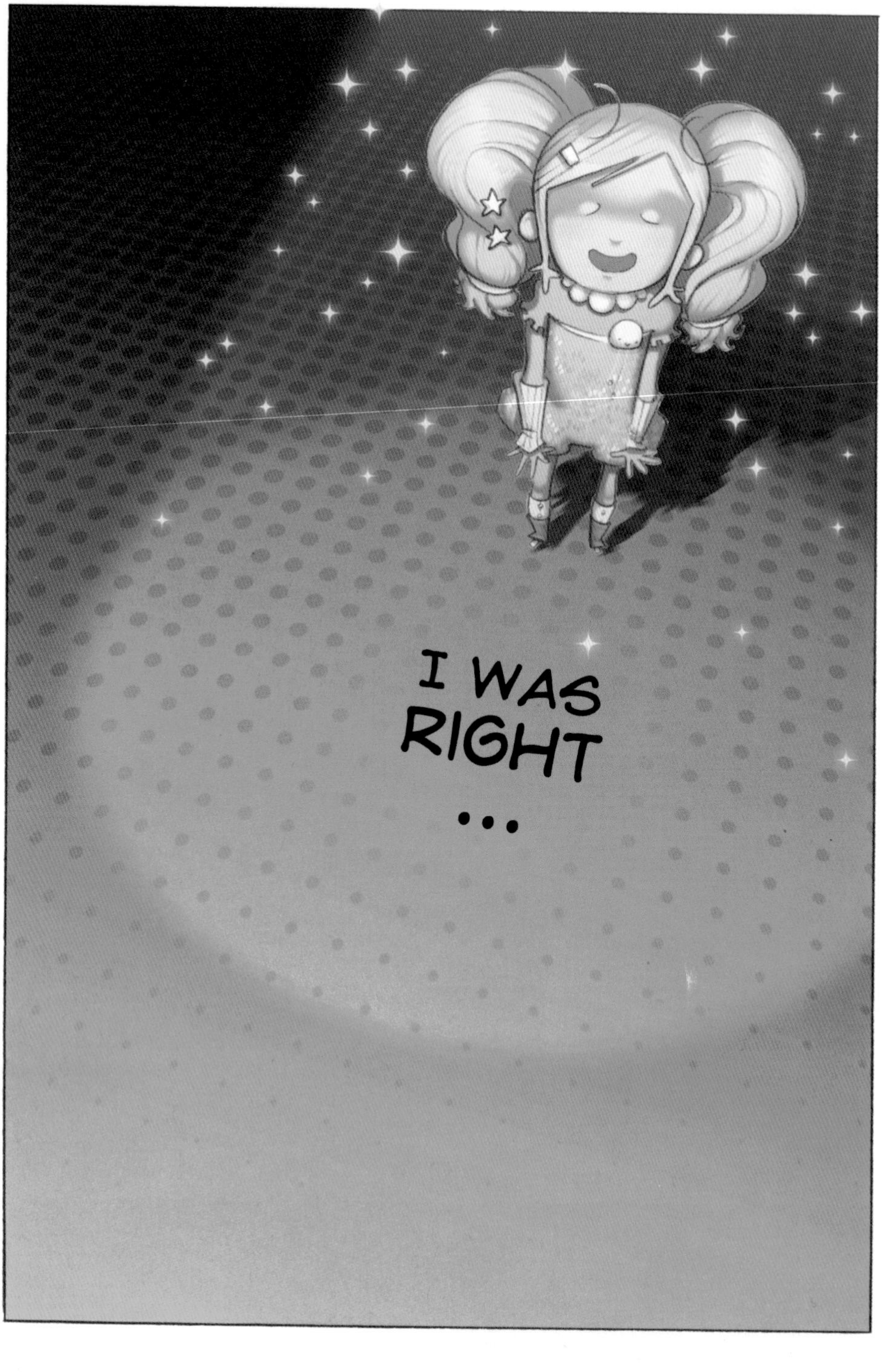
I WAS RIGHT . . .

Nola's Worlds #3

even for a dreamer like me

minikim ★ mariolle ★ pop

GRAPHIC UNIVERSE™ • MINNEAPOLIS • NEW YORK • LONDON

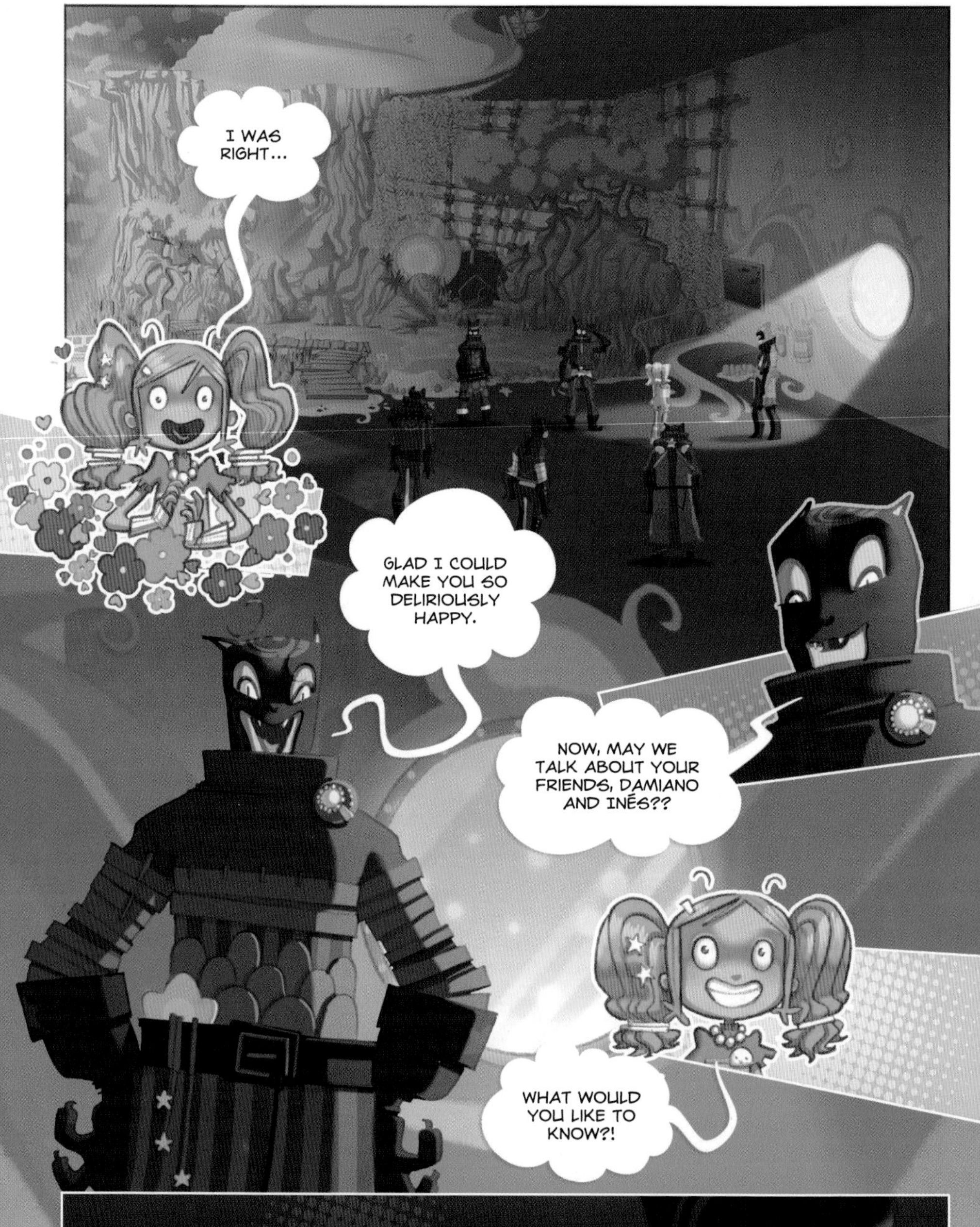
I WAS RIGHT...
GLAD I COULD MAKE YOU SO DELIRIOUSLY HAPPY.
NOW, MAY WE TALK ABOUT YOUR FRIENDS, DAMIANO AND INÉS??
WHAT WOULD YOU LIKE TO KNOW?!
EVERYTHING.

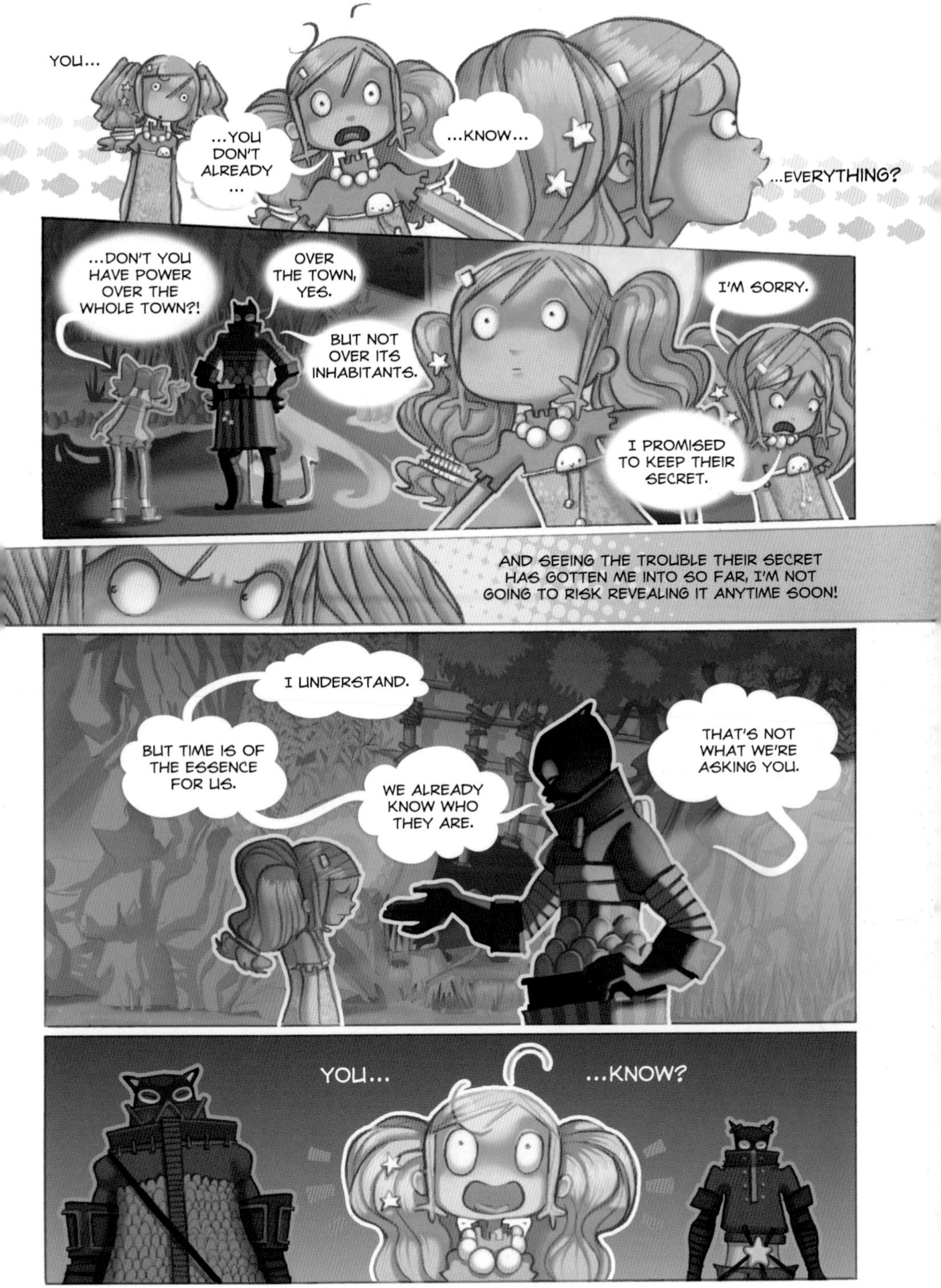
YOU...
...YOU DON'T ALREADY ...
...KNOW...
...EVERYTHING?
...DON'T YOU HAVE POWER OVER THE WHOLE TOWN?!
OVER THE TOWN, YES.
BUT NOT OVER ITS INHABITANTS.
I'M SORRY.
I PROMISED TO KEEP THEIR SECRET.
AND SEEING THE TROUBLE THEIR SECRET HAS GOTTEN ME INTO SO FAR, I'M NOT GOING TO RISK REVEALING IT ANYTIME SOON!
I UNDERSTAND.
BUT TIME IS OF THE ESSENCE FOR US.
WE ALREADY KNOW WHO THEY ARE.
THAT'S NOT WHAT WE'RE ASKING YOU.
YOU...
...KNOW?

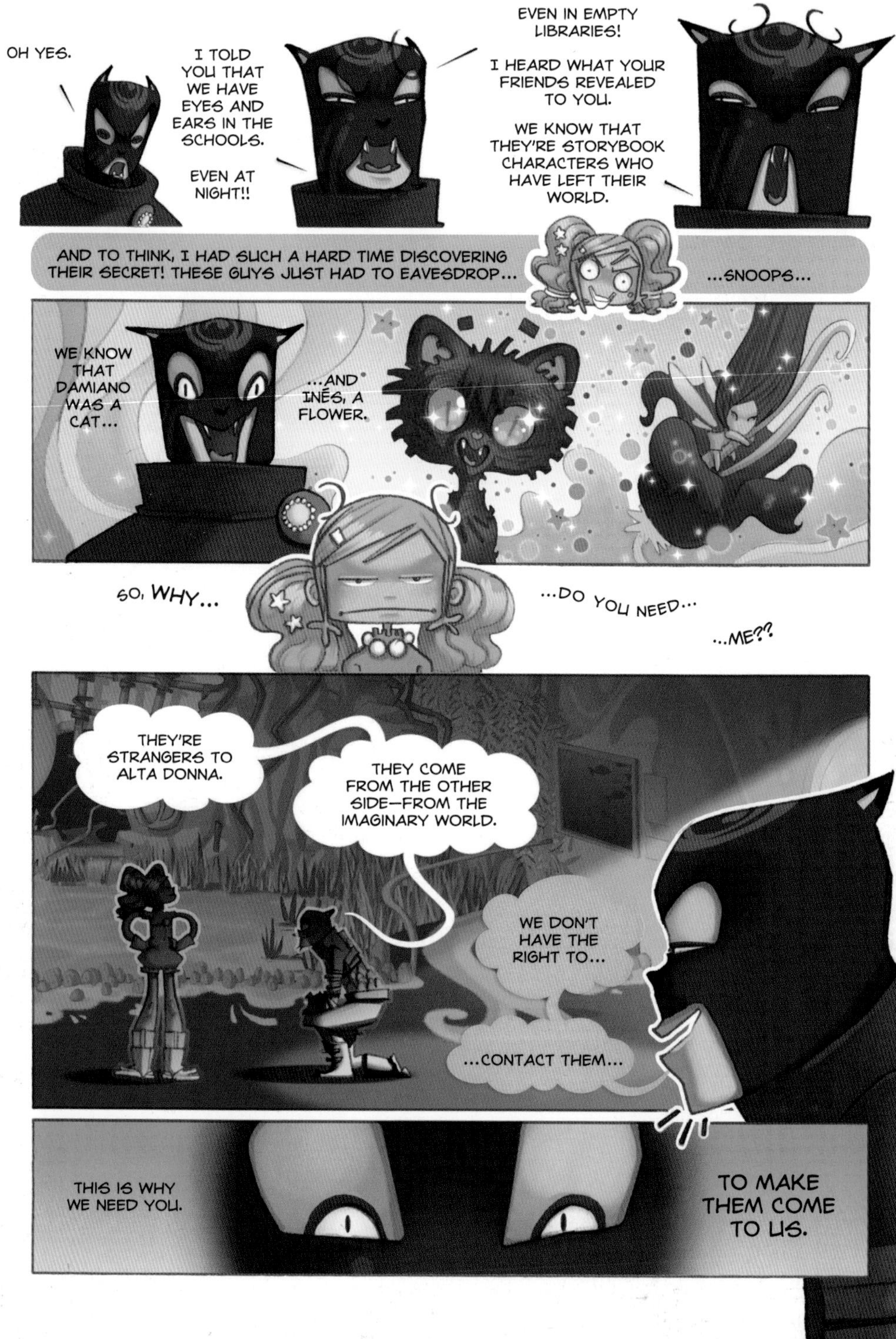

OH YES.
I TOLD YOU THAT WE HAVE EYES AND EARS IN THE SCHOOLS.
EVEN AT NIGHT!!
EVEN IN EMPTY LIBRARIES!
I HEARD WHAT YOUR FRIENDS REVEALED TO YOU.
WE KNOW THAT THEY'RE STORYBOOK CHARACTERS WHO HAVE LEFT THEIR WORLD.
AND TO THINK, I HAD SUCH A HARD TIME DISCOVERING THEIR SECRET! THESE GUYS JUST HAD TO EAVESDROP...
...SNOOPS...
WE KNOW THAT DAMIANO WAS A CAT...
...AND INÉS, A FLOWER.
SO, WHY...
...DO YOU NEED...
...ME??
THEY'RE STRANGERS TO ALTA DONNA.
THEY COME FROM THE OTHER SIDE—FROM THE IMAGINARY WORLD.
WE DON'T HAVE THE RIGHT TO...
...CONTACT THEM...
THIS IS WHY WE NEED YOU.
TO MAKE THEM COME TO US.

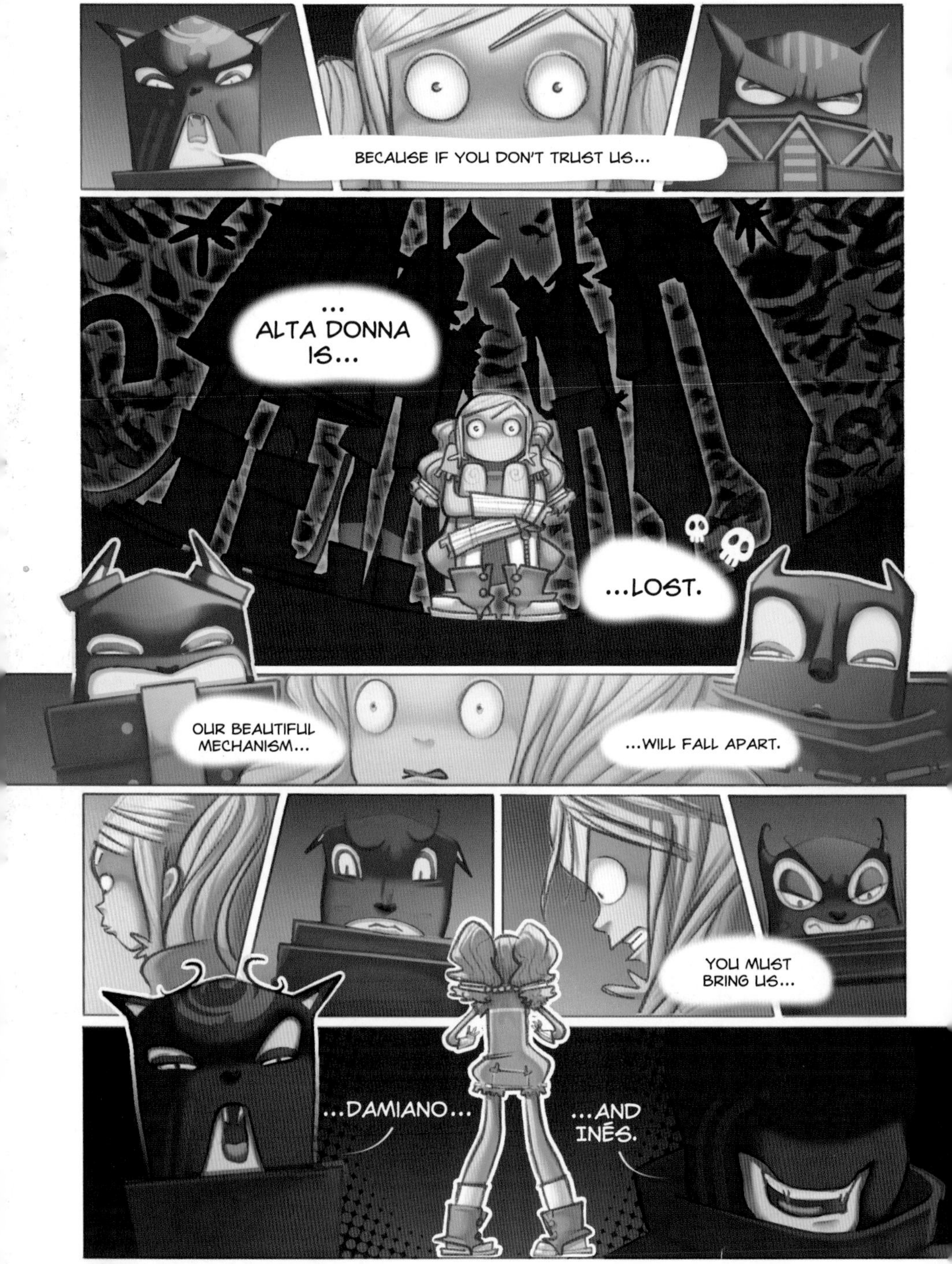
BECAUSE IF YOU DON'T TRUST US...
... ALTA DONNA IS...
...LOST.
OUR BEAUTIFUL MECHANISM...
...WILL FALL APART.
YOU MUST BRING US...
...DAMIANO...
...AND INÉS.

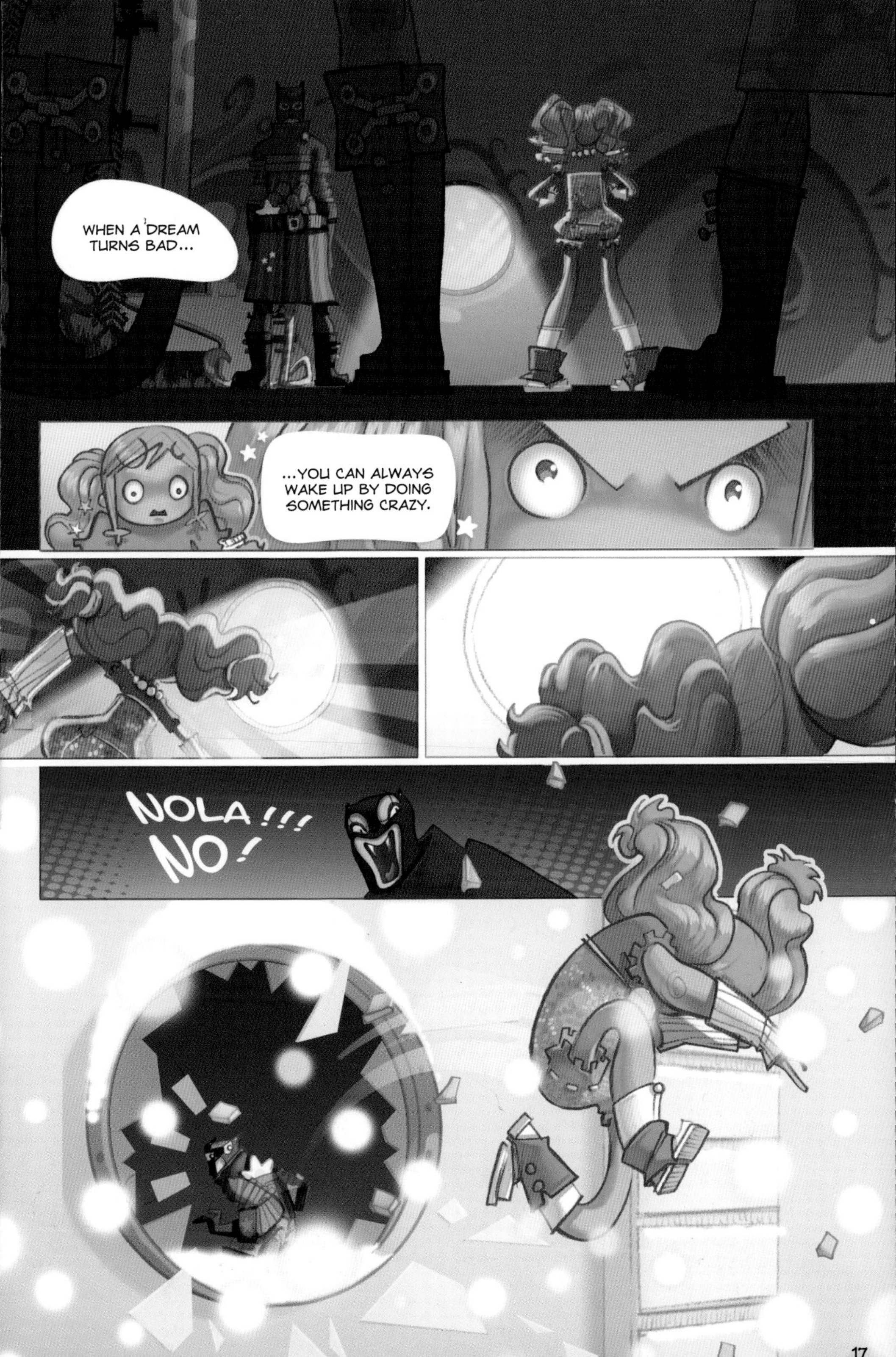
WHEN A DREAM TURNS BAD...
...YOU CAN ALWAYS WAKE UP BY DOING SOMETHING CRAZY.
NOLA!!! NO!

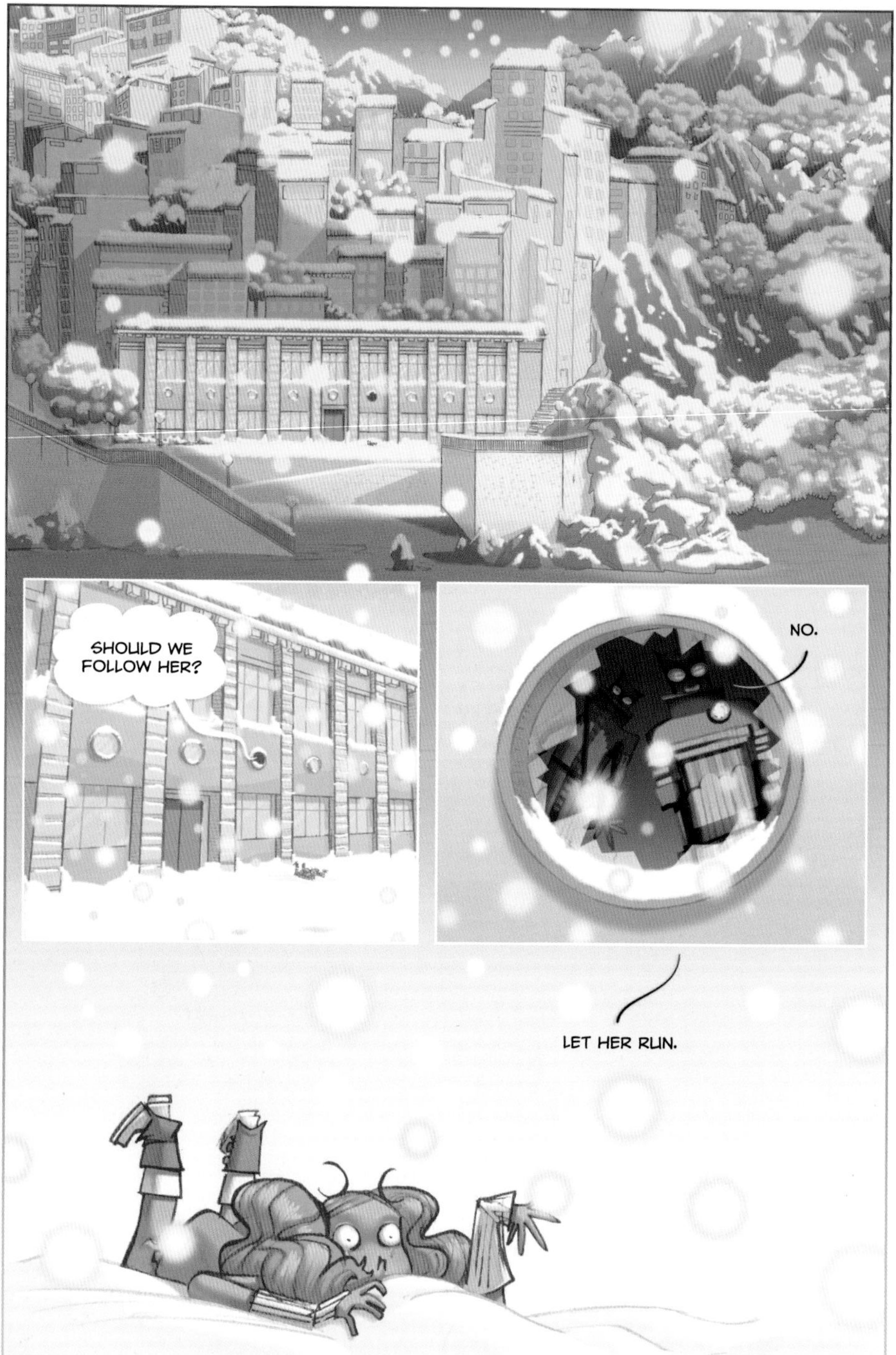
SHOULD WE FOLLOW HER?
NO.
LET HER RUN.

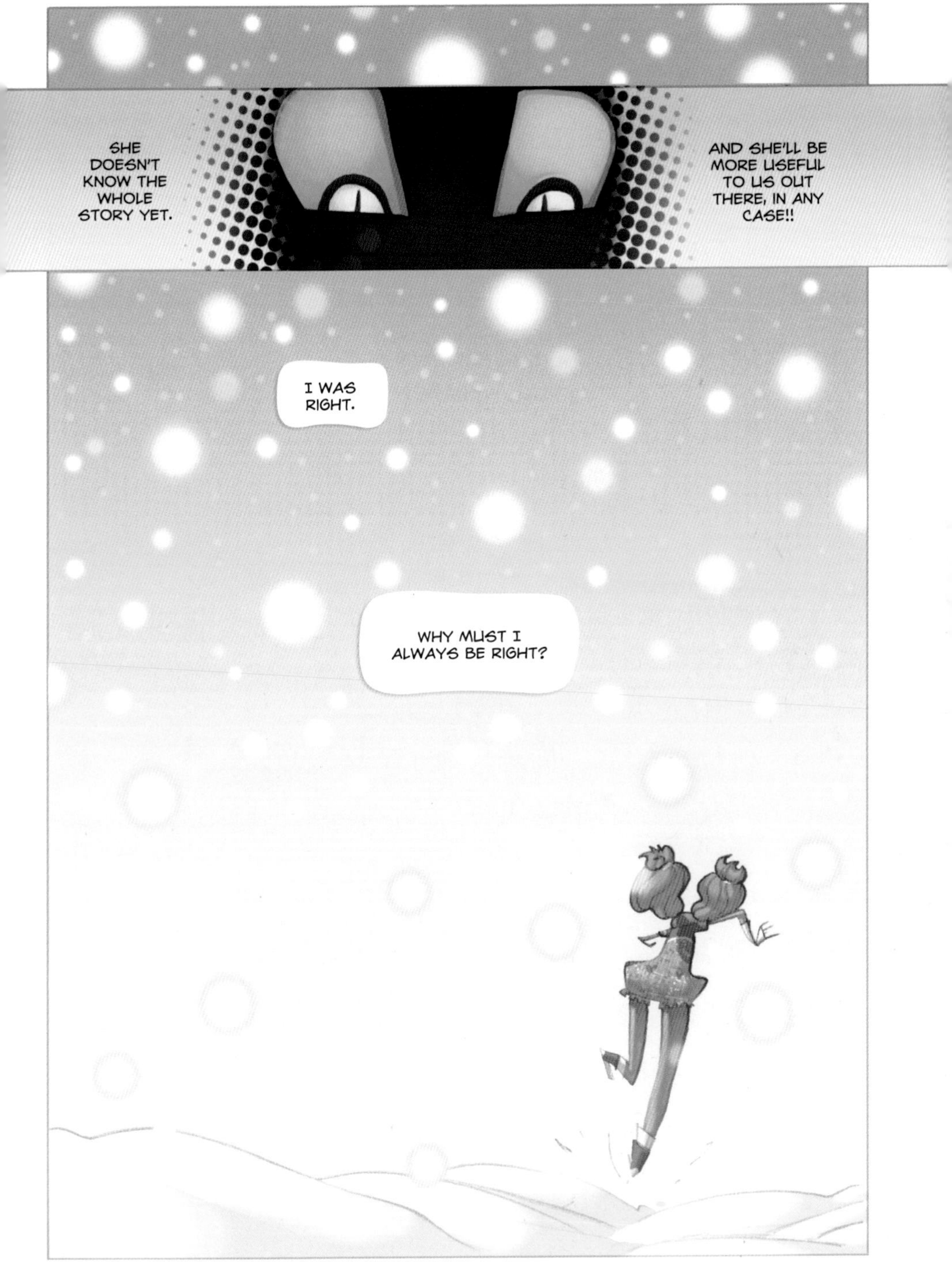
SHE DOESN'T KNOW THE WHOLE STORY YET.
AND SHE'LL BE MORE USEFUL TO US OUT THERE, IN ANY CASE!!
I WAS RIGHT.
WHY MUST I ALWAYS BE RIGHT?

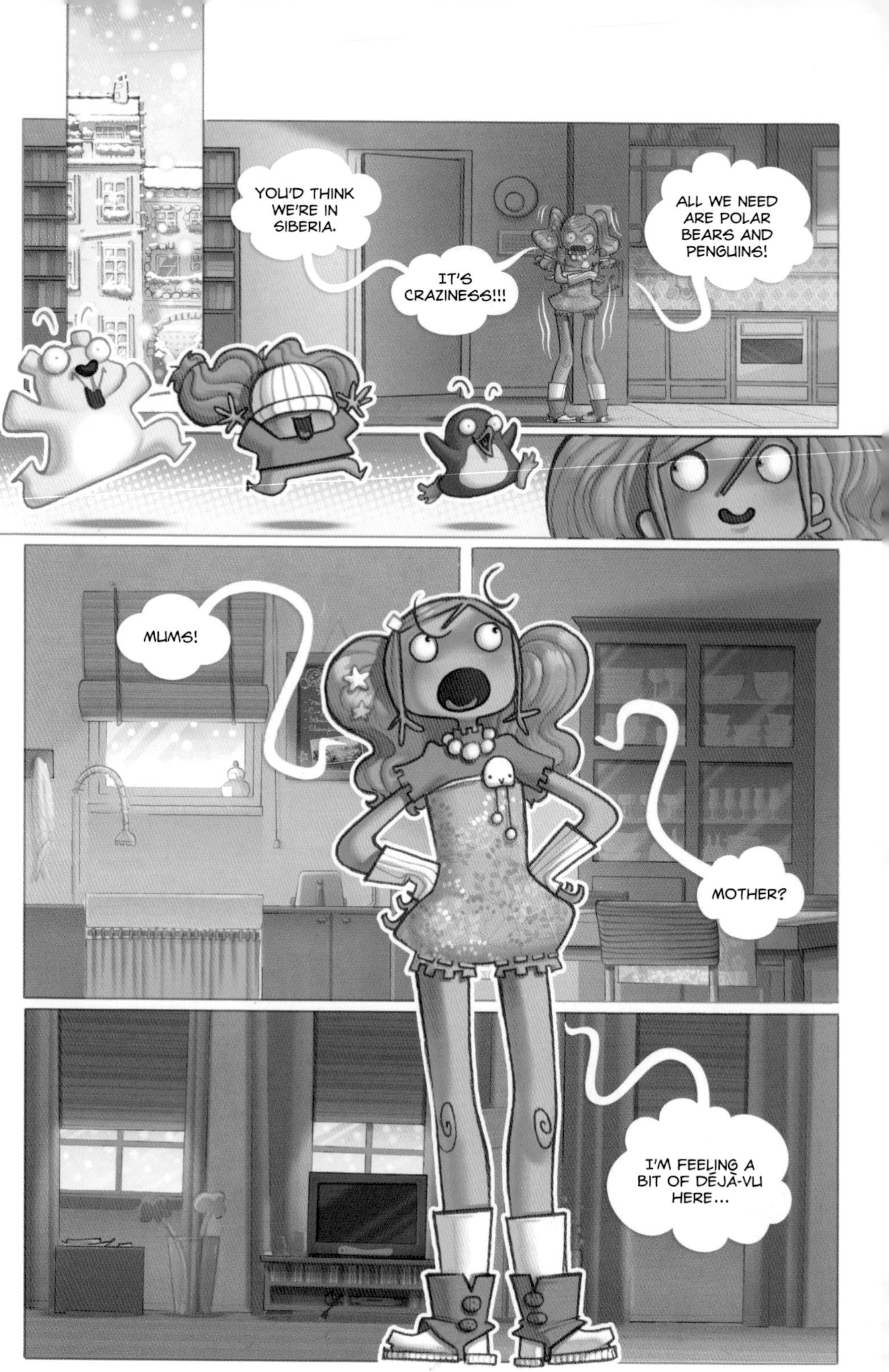
YOU'D THINK WE'RE IN SIBERIA.
IT'S CRAZINESS!!!
ALL WE NEED ARE POLAR BEARS AND PENGUINS!
MUMS!
MOTHER?
I'M FEELING A BIT OF DÉJÀ-VU HERE...

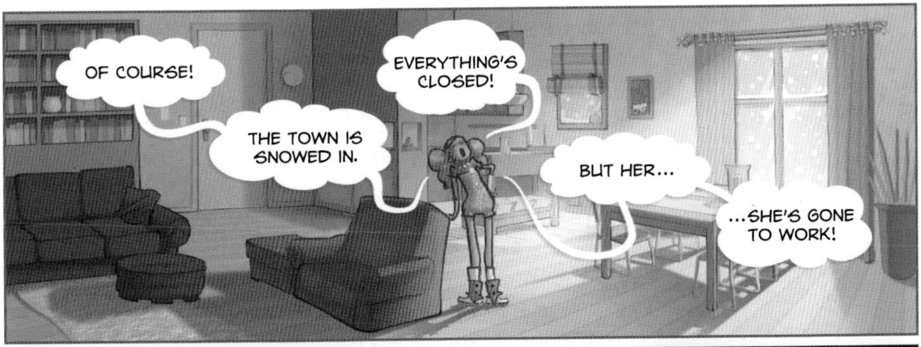
OF COURSE!
THE TOWN IS SNOWED IN.
EVERYTHING'S CLOSED!
BUT HER...
...SHE'S GONE TO WORK!

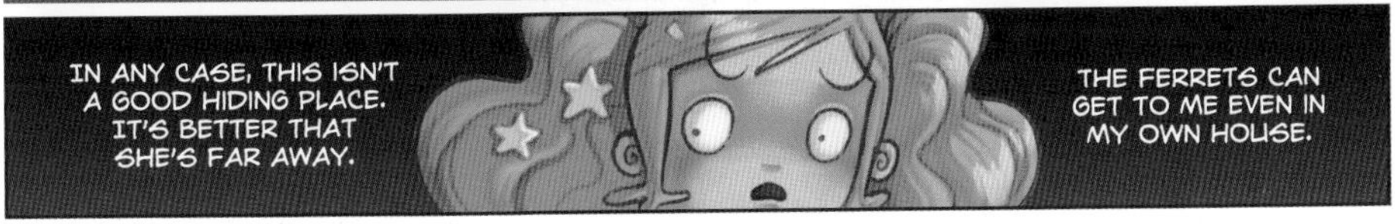
IN ANY CASE, THIS ISN'T A GOOD HIDING PLACE. IT'S BETTER THAT SHE'S FAR AWAY.
THE FERRETS CAN GET TO ME EVEN IN MY OWN HOUSE.

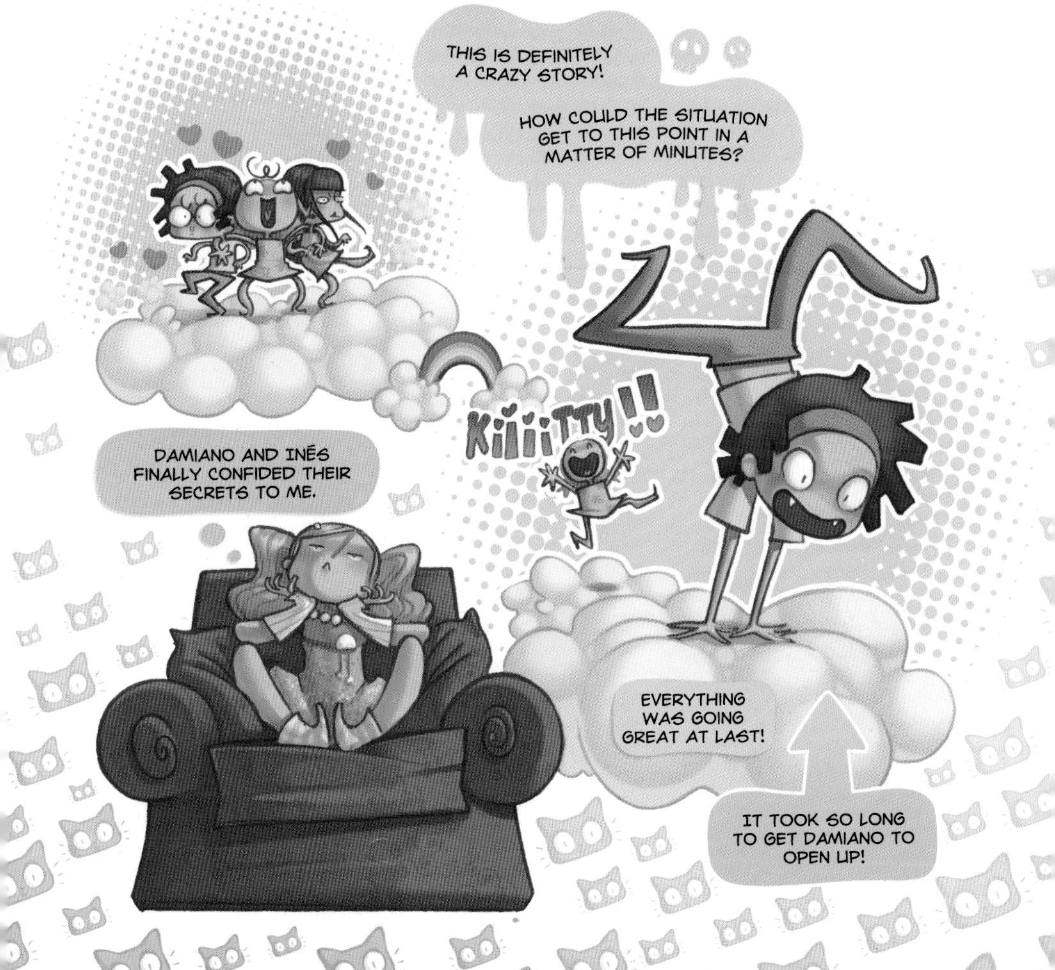
THIS IS DEFINITELY A CRAZY STORY!
HOW COULD THE SITUATION GET TO THIS POINT IN A MATTER OF MINUTES?
DAMIANO AND INÉS FINALLY CONFIDED THEIR SECRETS TO ME.
KIIIITTY!!
EVERYTHING WAS GOING GREAT AT LAST!
IT TOOK SO LONG TO GET DAMIANO TO OPEN UP!

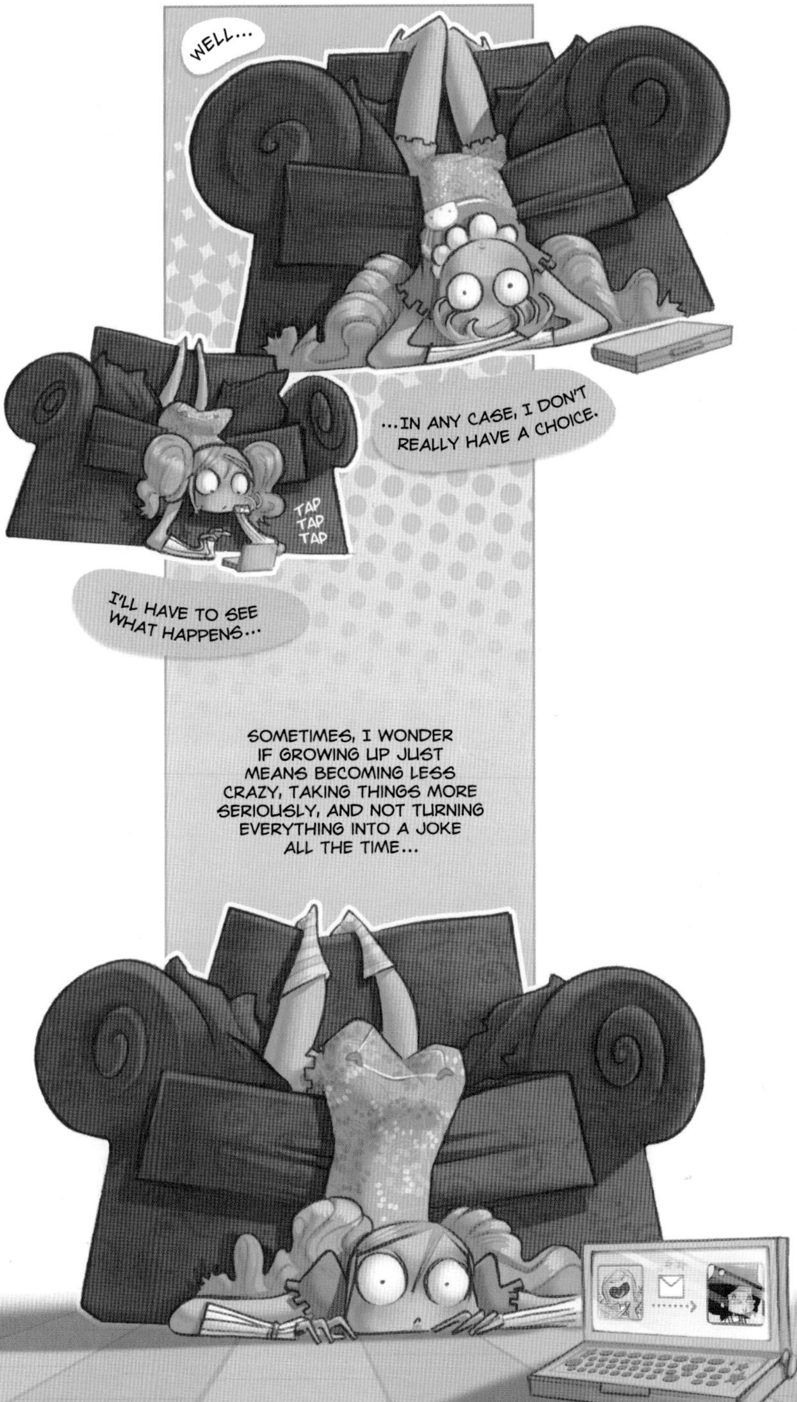
WELL...
...IN ANY CASE, I DON'T REALLY HAVE A CHOICE.
TAP TAP TAP
I'LL HAVE TO SEE WHAT HAPPENS...
SOMETIMES, I WONDER IF GROWING UP JUST MEANS BECOMING LESS CRAZY, TAKING THINGS MORE SERIOUSLY, AND NOT TURNING EVERYTHING INTO A JOKE ALL THE TIME...

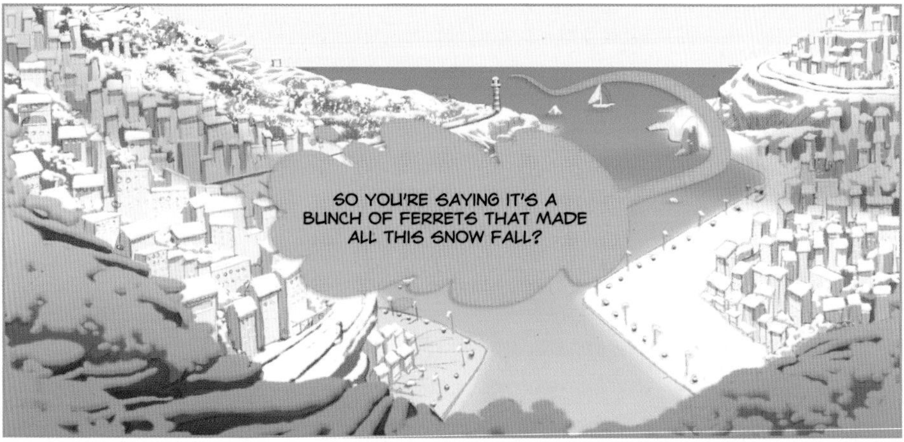
SO YOU'RE SAYING IT'S A BUNCH OF FERRETS THAT MADE ALL THIS SNOW FALL?

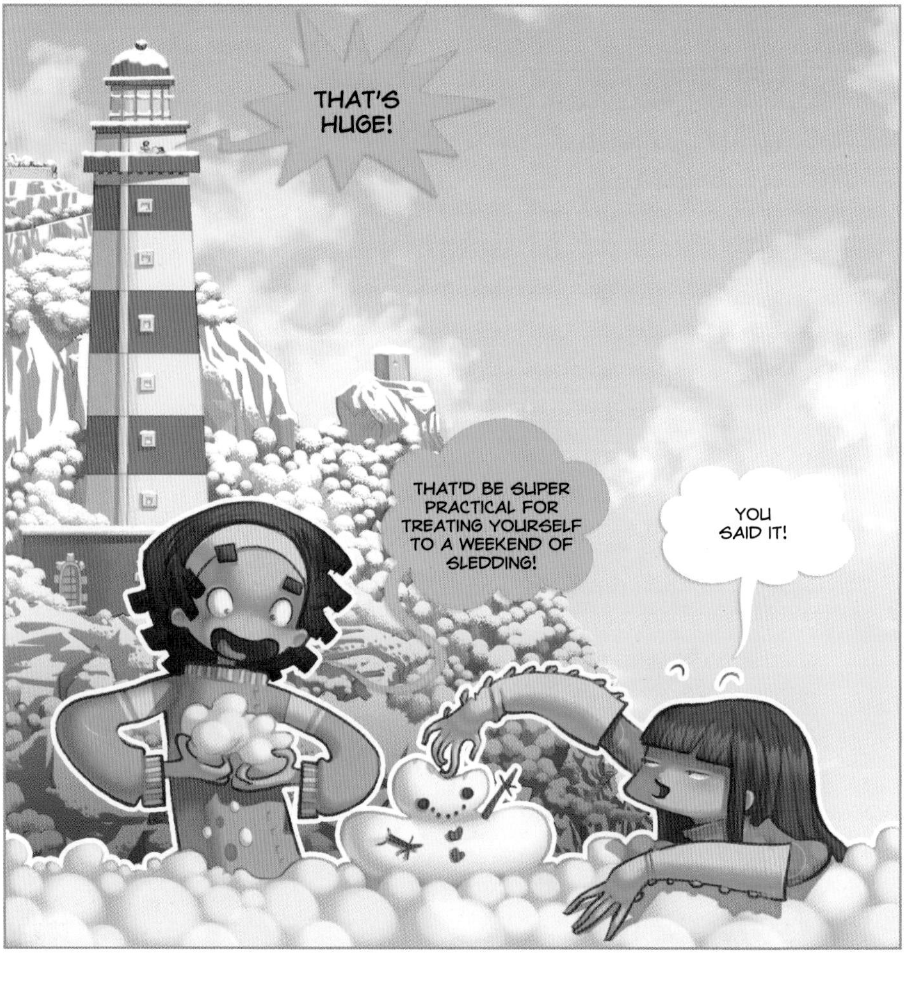
THAT'S HUGE!
THAT'D BE SUPER PRACTICAL FOR TREATING YOURSELF TO A WEEKEND OF SLEDDING!
YOU SAID IT!

25

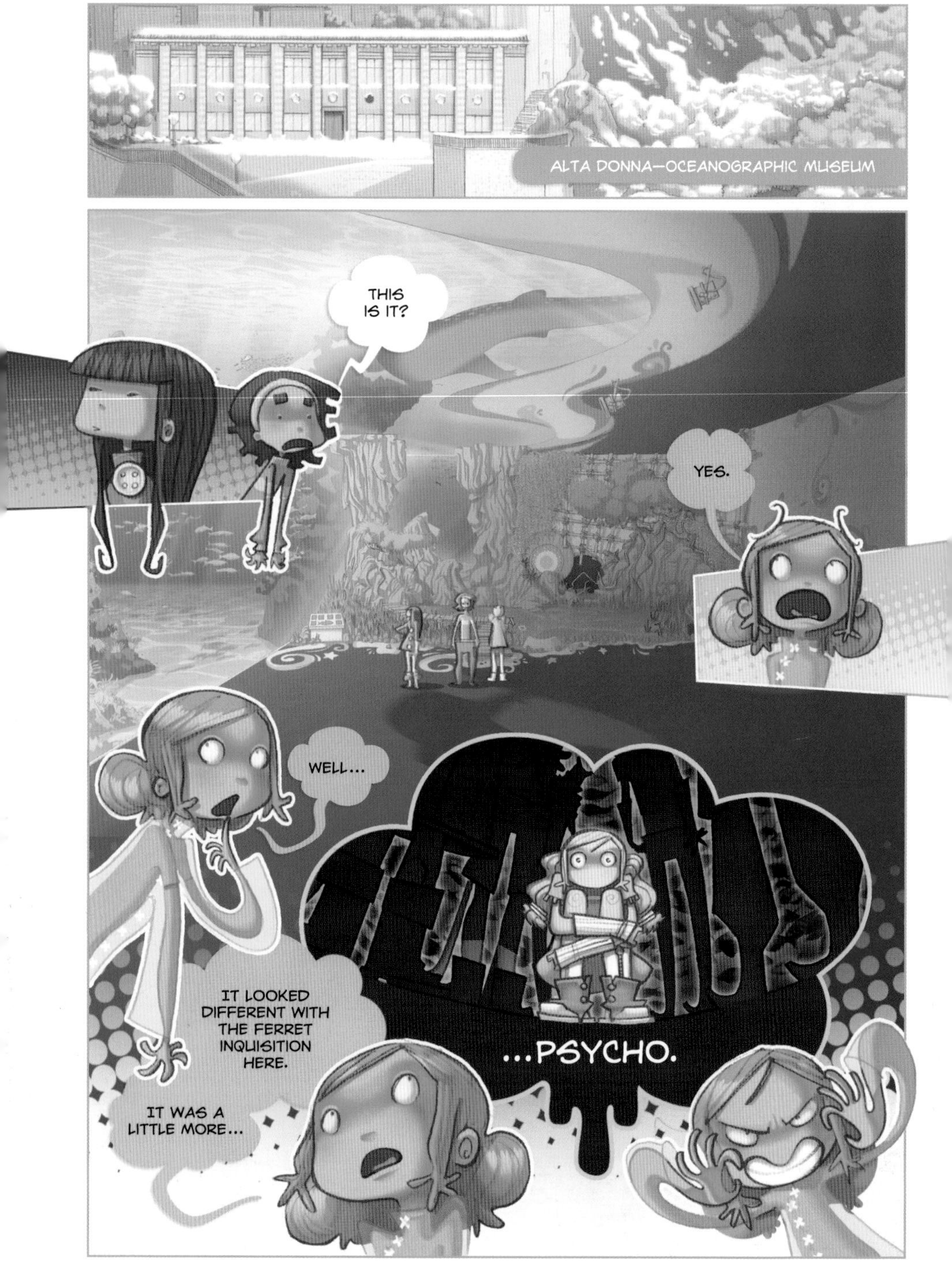
ALTA DONNA—OCEANOGRAPHIC MUSEUM
THIS IS IT?
YES.
WELL...
IT LOOKED DIFFERENT WITH THE FERRET INQUISITION HERE.
IT WAS A LITTLE MORE...
...PSYCHO.

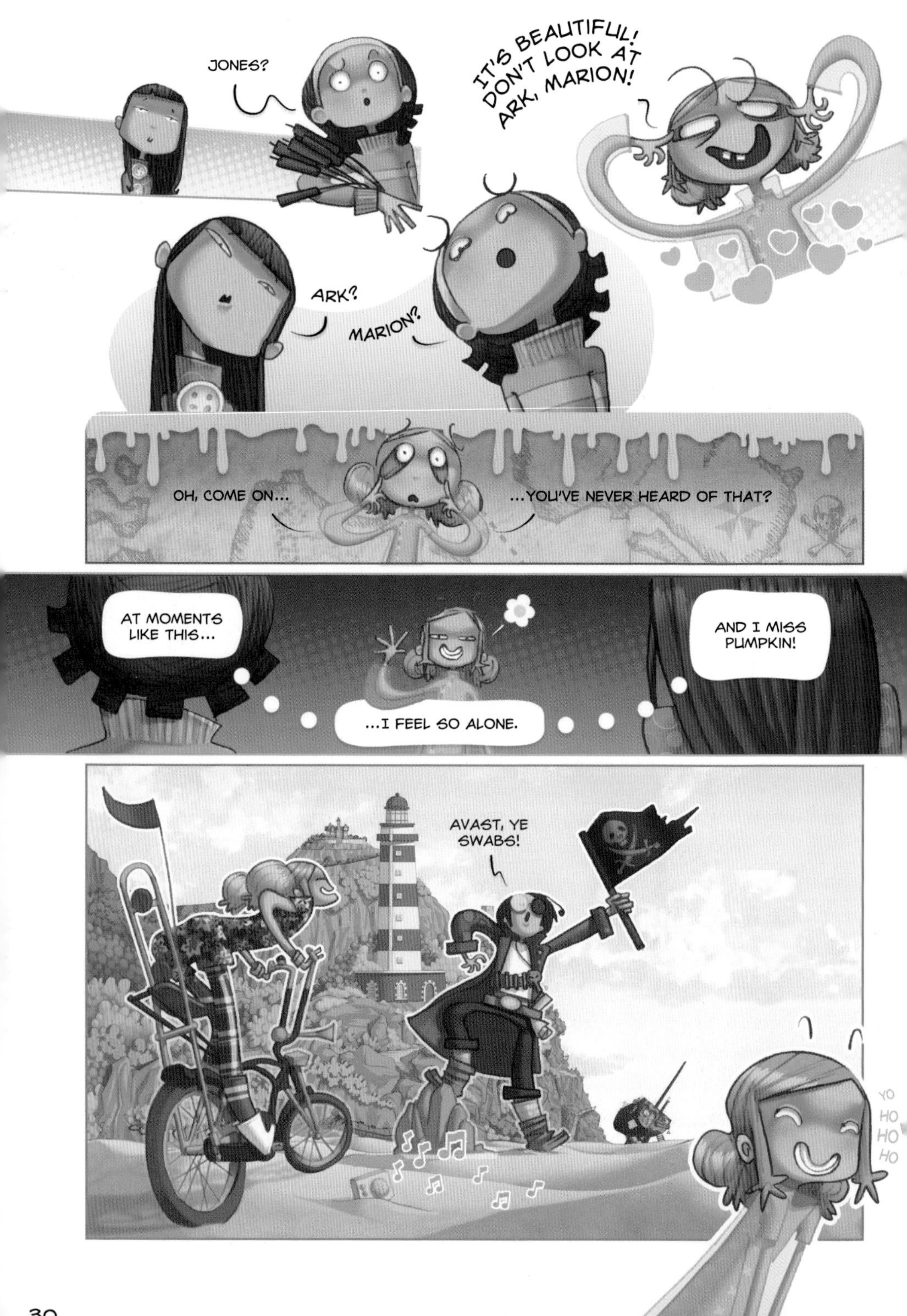
JONES?
IT'S BEAUTIFUL! DON'T LOOK AT ARK, MARION!
ARK?
MARION?
OH, COME ON...
...YOU'VE NEVER HEARD OF THAT?
AT MOMENTS LIKE THIS...
...I FEEL SO ALONE.
AND I MISS PUMPKIN!
AVAST, YE SWABS!
YO HO HO HO

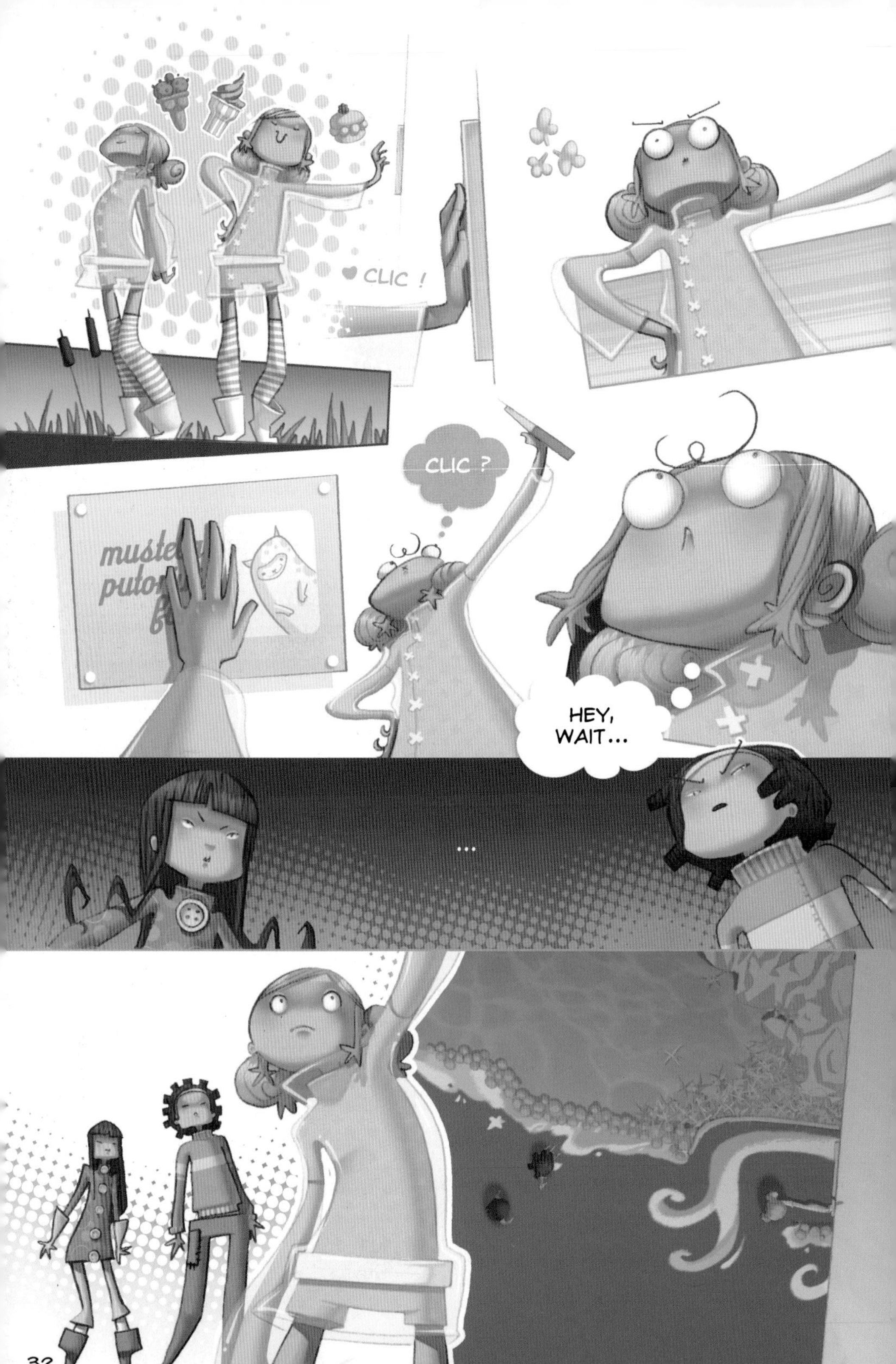

CLIC !
CLIC ?
HEY, WAIT...
...

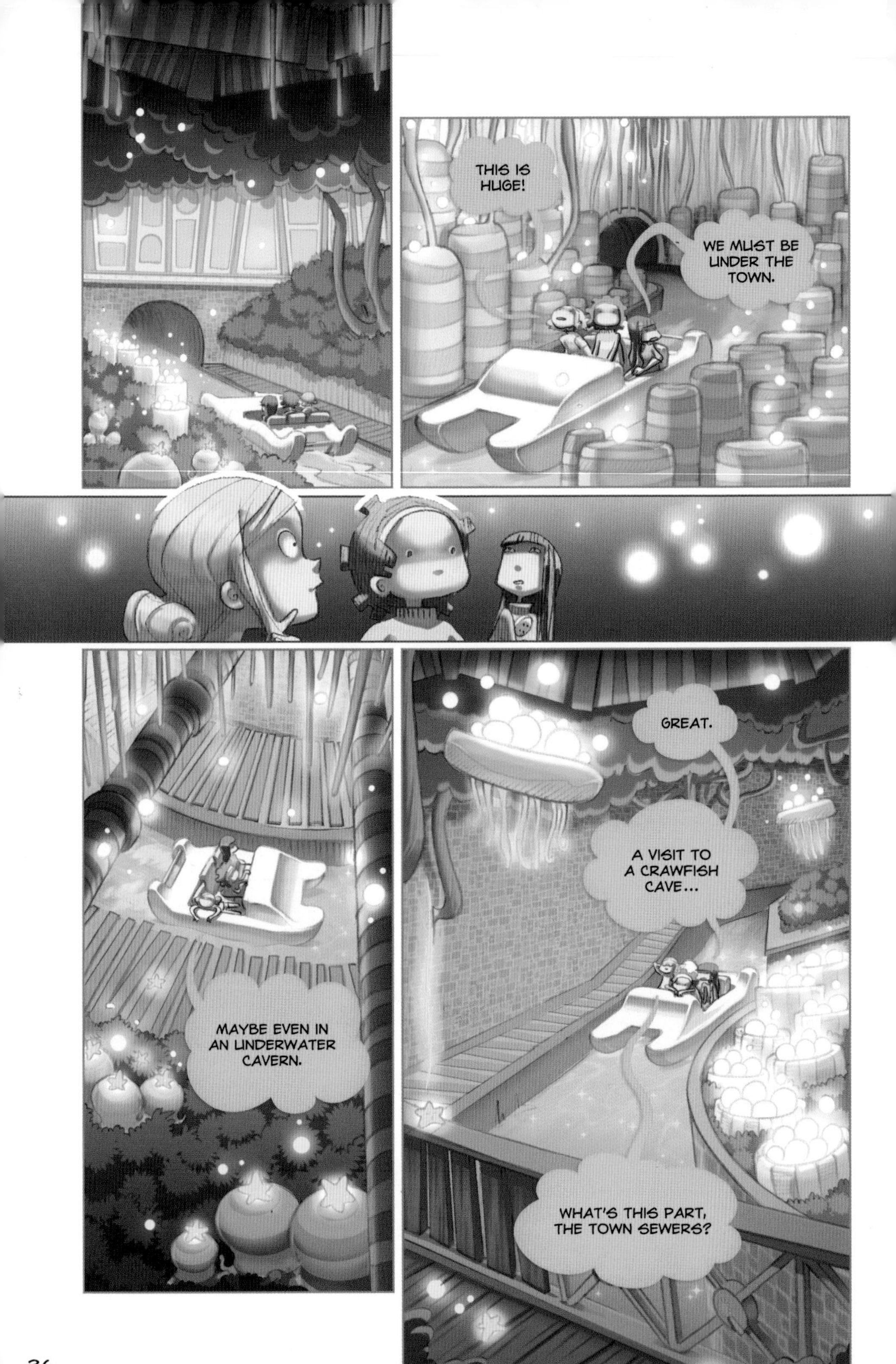
THIS IS HUGE!
WE MUST BE UNDER THE TOWN.
GREAT.
A VISIT TO A CRAWFISH CAVE...
MAYBE EVEN IN AN UNDERWATER CAVERN.
WHAT'S THIS PART, THE TOWN SEWERS?

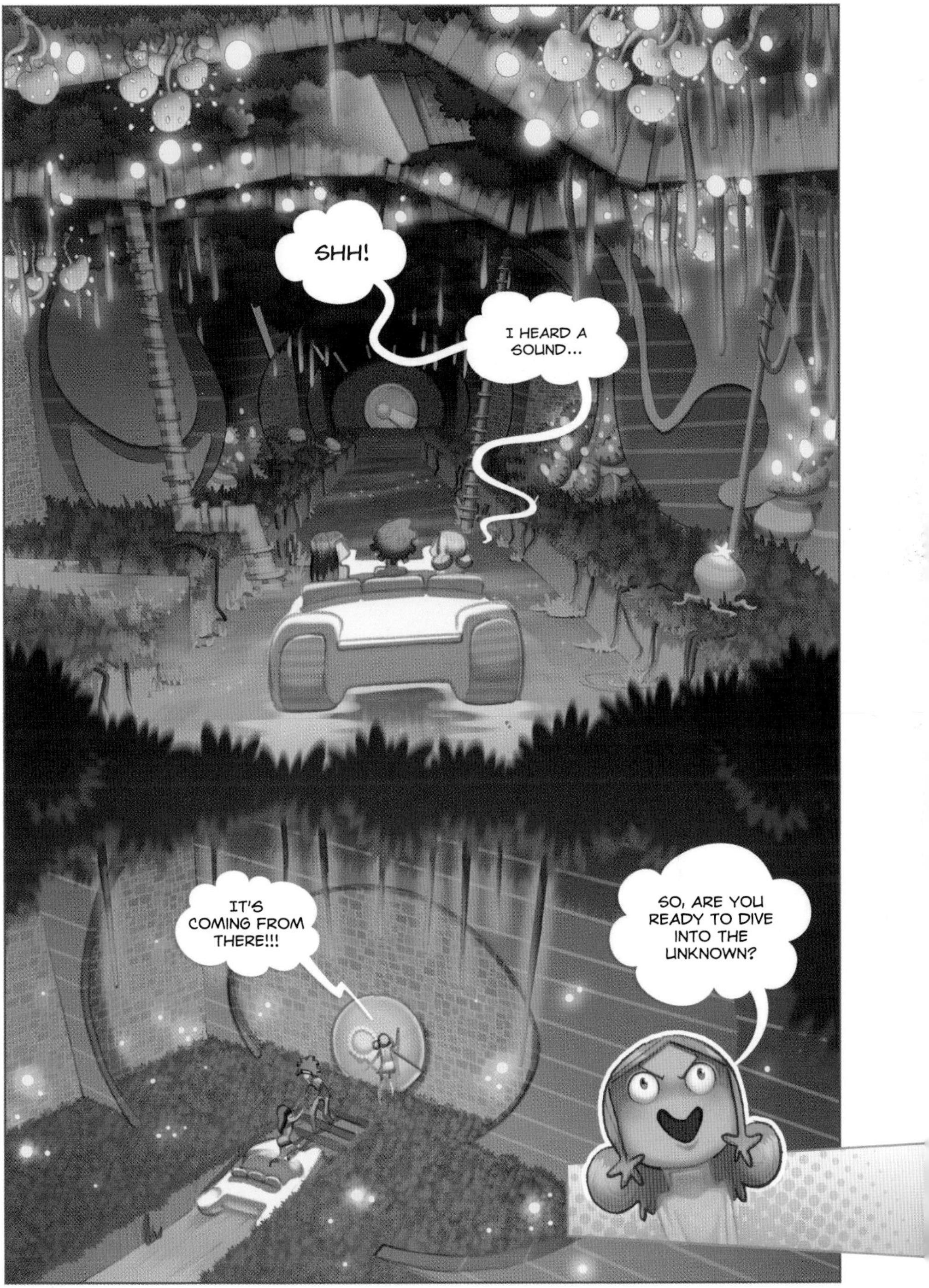
SHH!
I HEARD A SOUND...
IT'S COMING FROM THERE!!!
SO, ARE YOU READY TO DIVE INTO THE UNKNOWN?

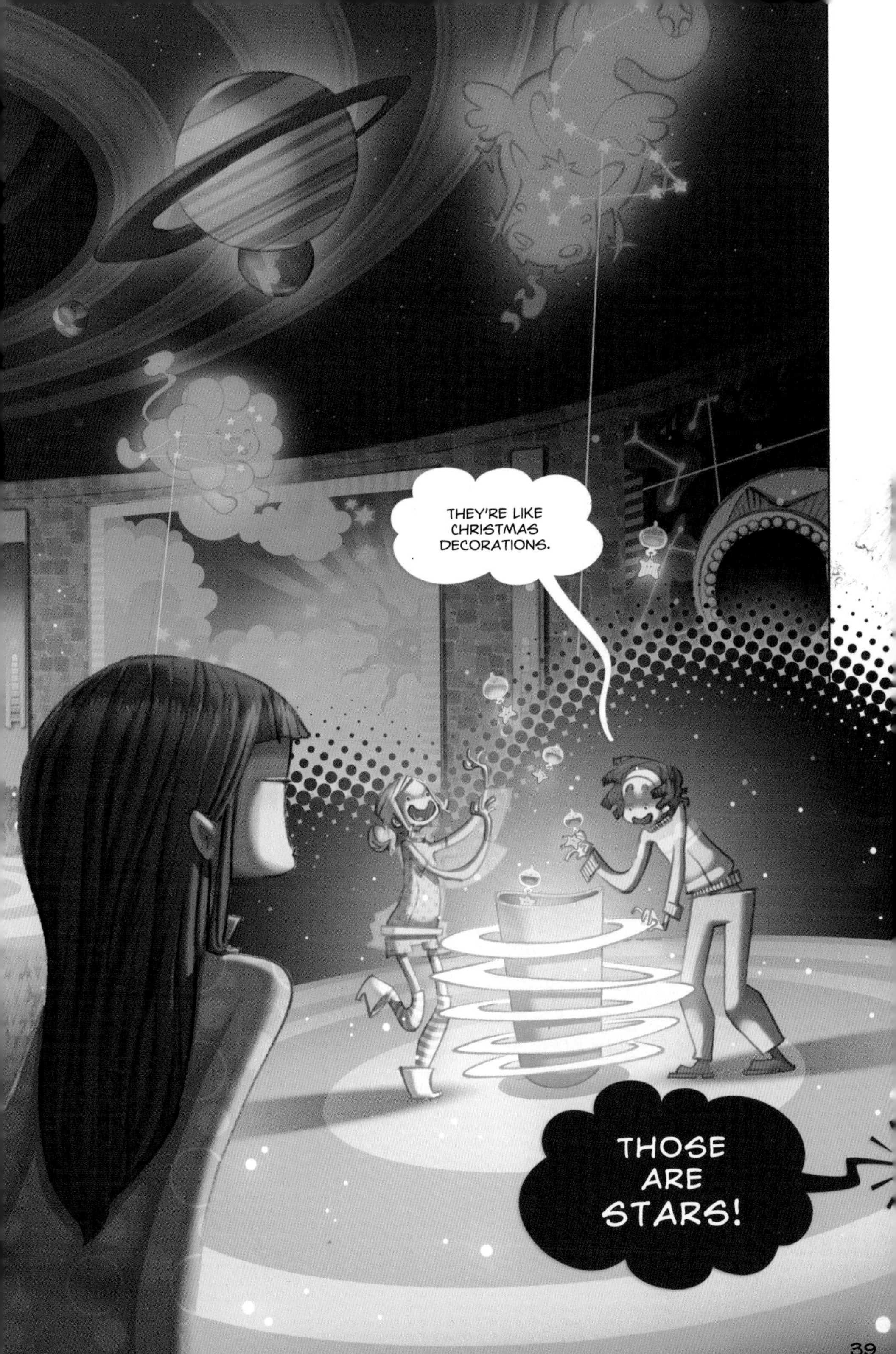
THEY'RE LIKE CHRISTMAS DECORATIONS.
THOSE ARE STARS!

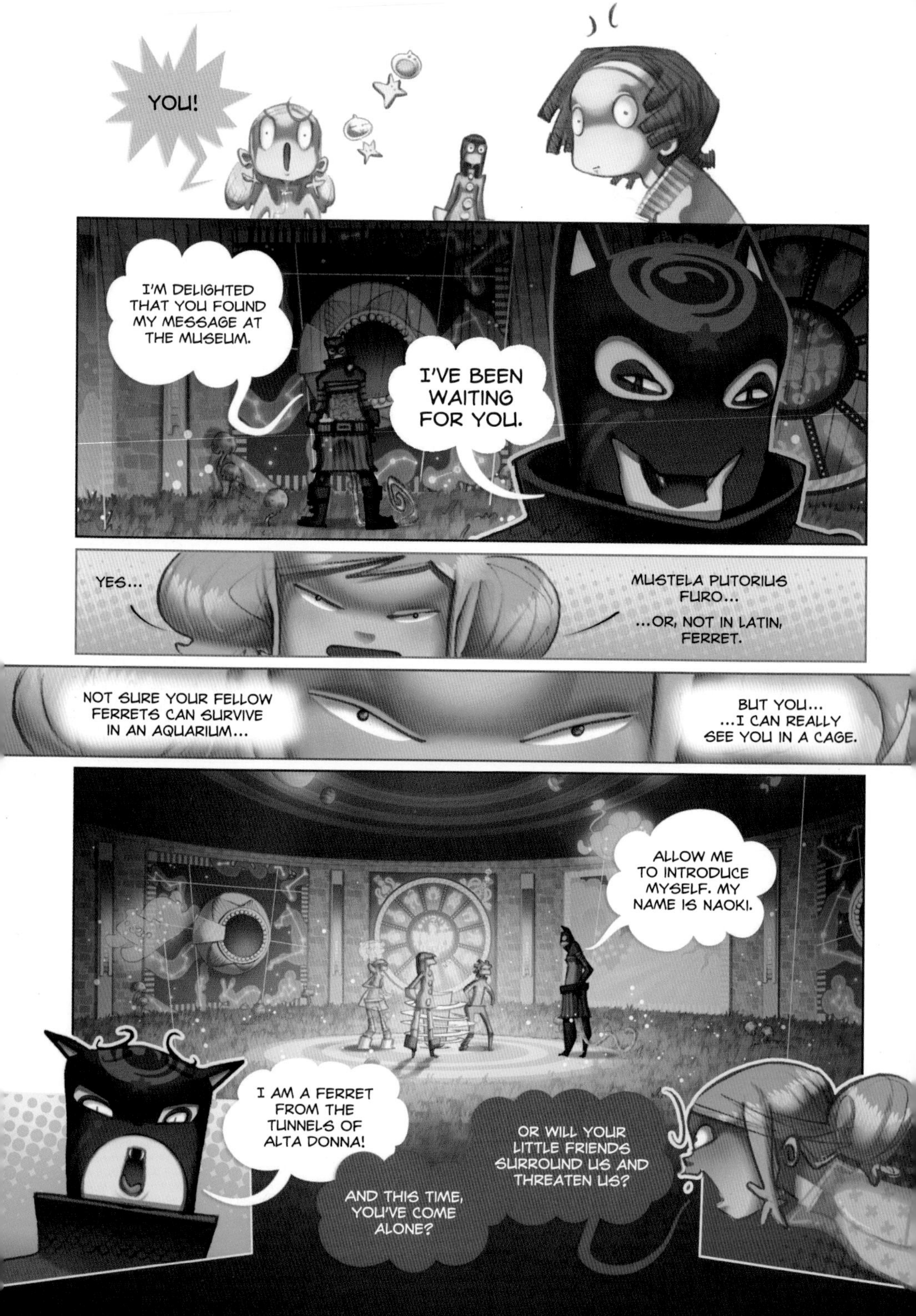
YOU!
I'M DELIGHTED THAT YOU FOUND MY MESSAGE AT THE MUSEUM.
I'VE BEEN WAITING FOR YOU.
YES...
MUSTELA PUTORIUS FURO...
...OR, NOT IN LATIN, FERRET.
NOT SURE YOUR FELLOW FERRETS CAN SURVIVE IN AN AQUARIUM...
BUT YOU... ...I CAN REALLY SEE YOU IN A CAGE.
ALLOW ME TO INTRODUCE MYSELF. MY NAME IS NAOKI.
I AM A FERRET FROM THE TUNNELS OF ALTA DONNA!
AND THIS TIME, YOU'VE COME ALONE?
OR WILL YOUR LITTLE FRIENDS SURROUND US AND THREATEN US?

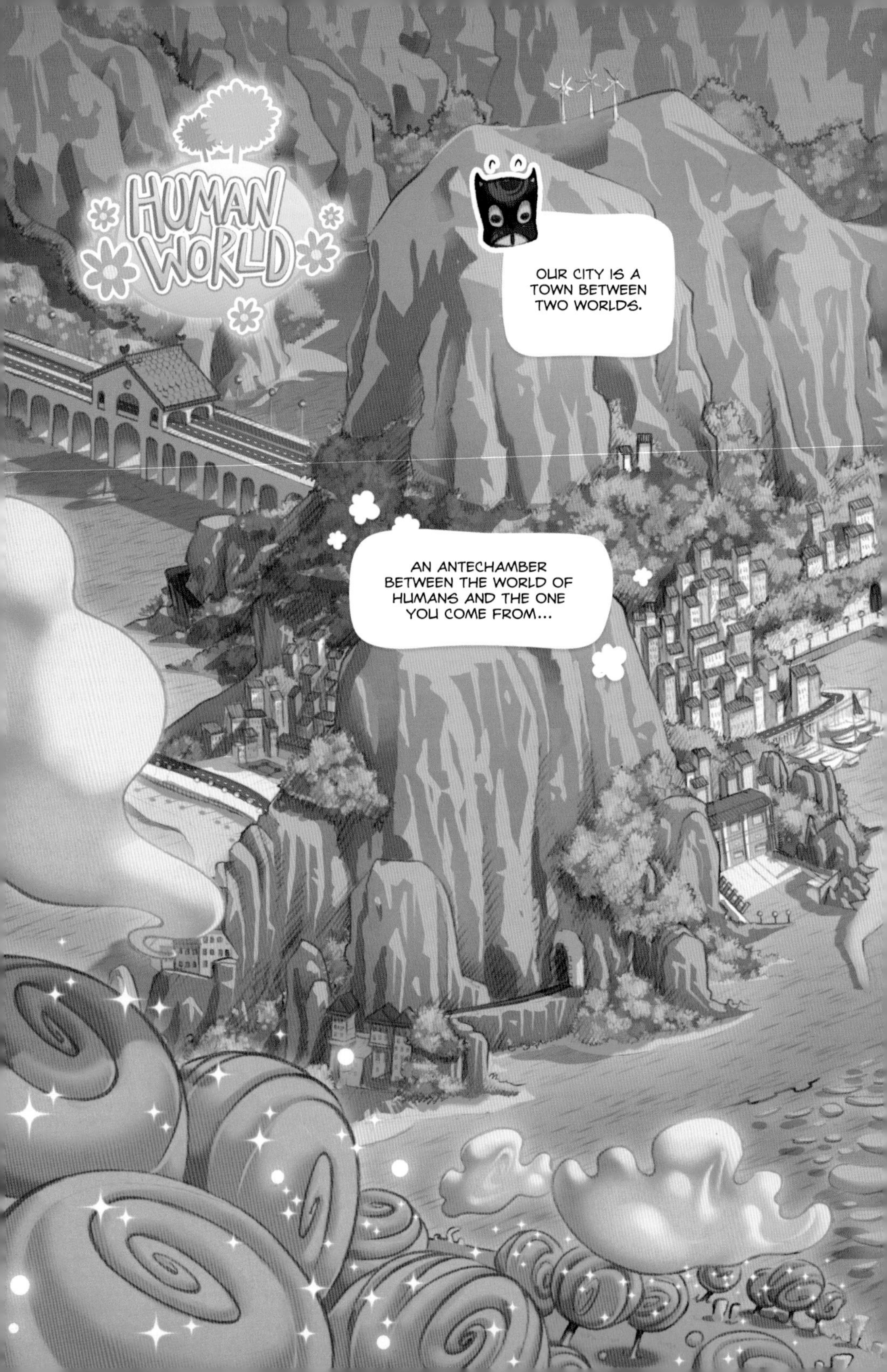
HUMAN WORLD
OUR CITY IS A TOWN BETWEEN TWO WORLDS.
AN ANTECHAMBER BETWEEN THE WORLD OF HUMANS AND THE ONE YOU COME FROM...

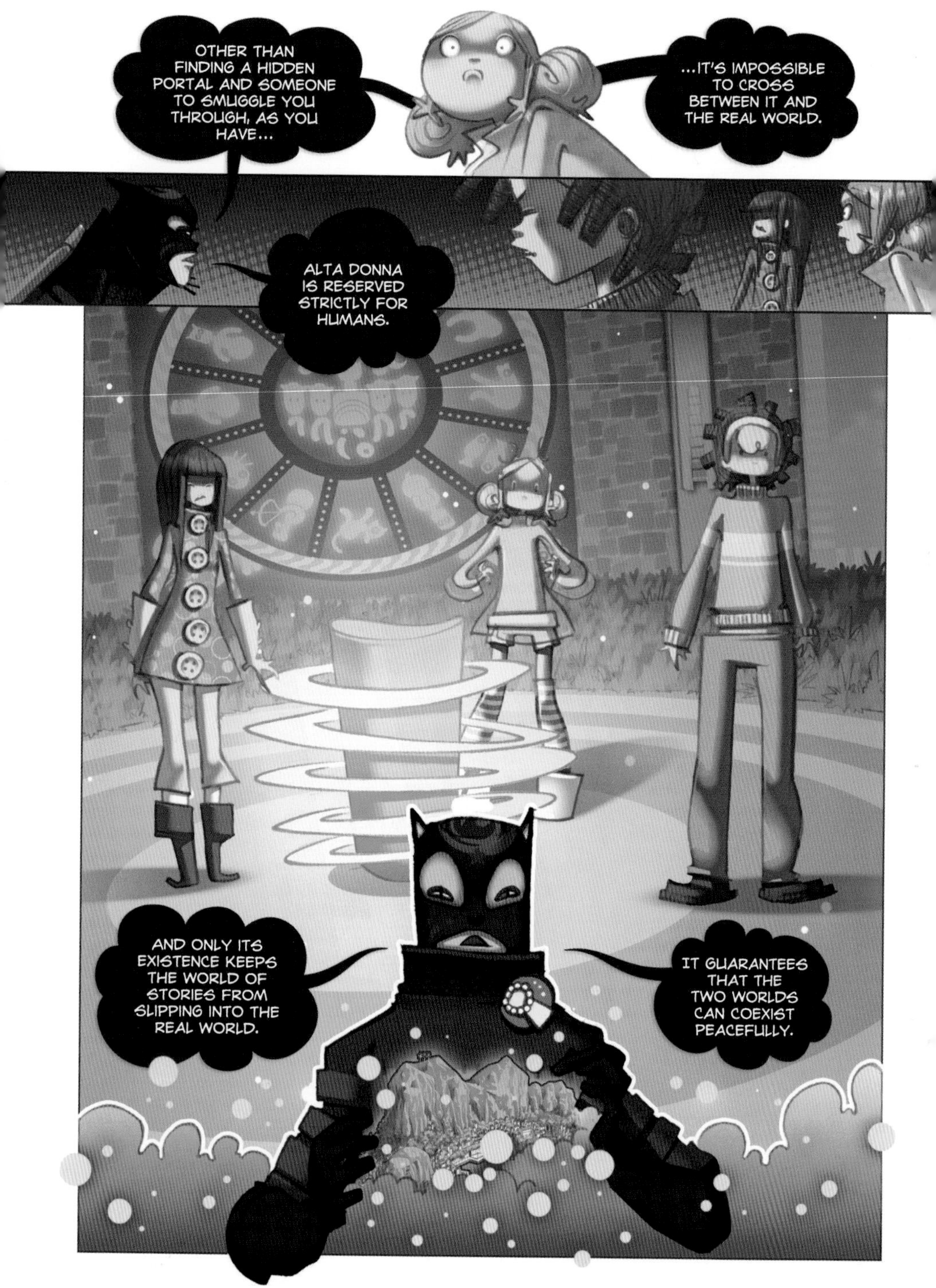
OTHER THAN FINDING A HIDDEN PORTAL AND SOMEONE TO SMUGGLE YOU THROUGH, AS YOU HAVE...
...IT'S IMPOSSIBLE TO CROSS BETWEEN IT AND THE REAL WORLD.
ALTA DONNA IS RESERVED STRICTLY FOR HUMANS.
AND ONLY ITS EXISTENCE KEEPS THE WORLD OF STORIES FROM SLIPPING INTO THE REAL WORLD.
IT GUARANTEES THAT THE TWO WORLDS CAN COEXIST PEACEFULLY.

47

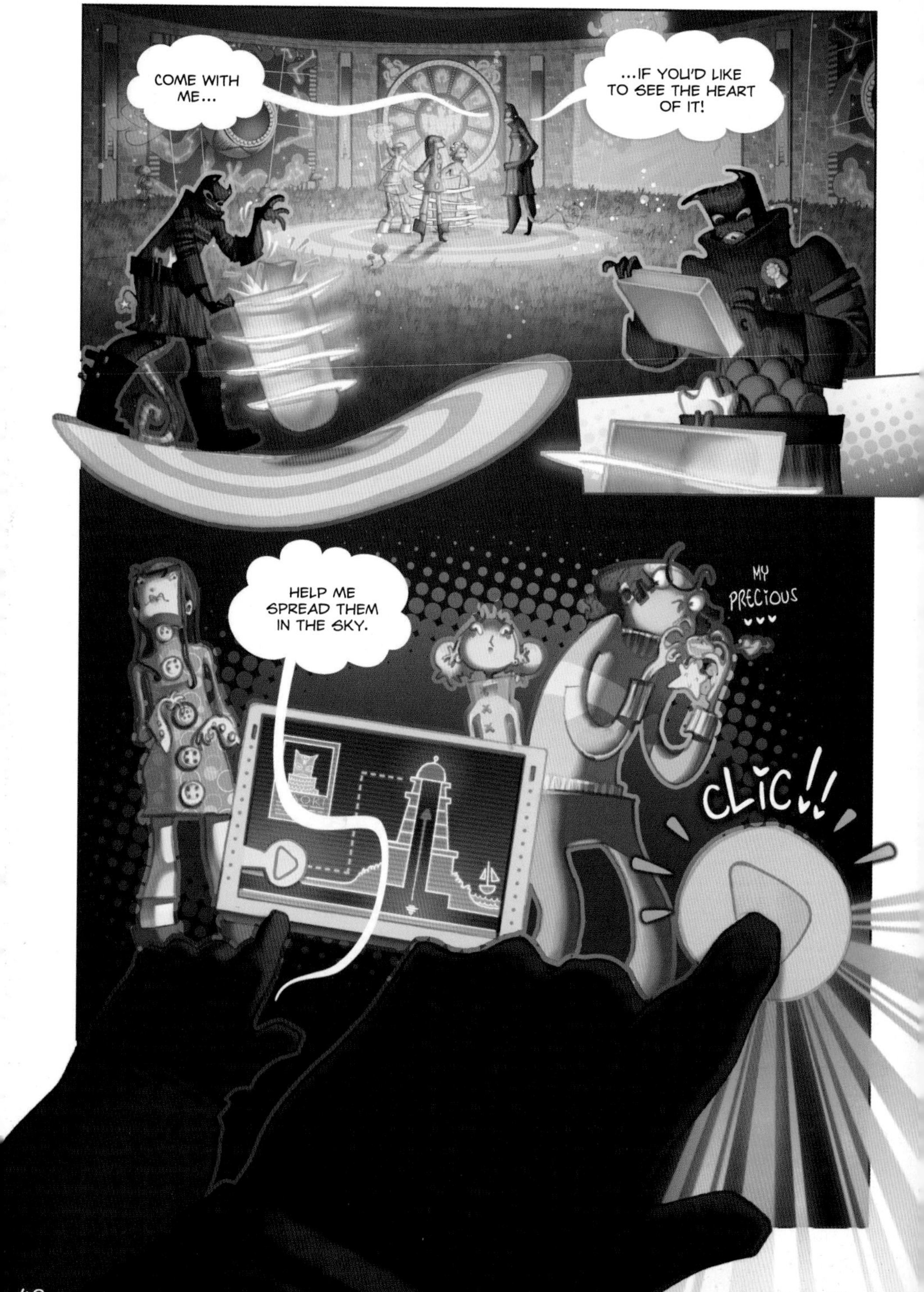
COME WITH ME...
...IF YOU'D LIKE TO SEE THE HEART OF IT!
HELP ME SPREAD THEM IN THE SKY.
MY PRECIOUS
CLIC!!

WoOow!
WE CLIMBED DOWN THAT ENDLESS LADDER AND FOLLOWED THOSE DAMP CORRIDORS WHEN THERE WAS AN ELEVATOR?
THAT WOULDN'T HAVE BEEN AS FUN!
IT'S THE HUNT THAT COUNTS, NOT FINDING THE TREASURE CHEST...

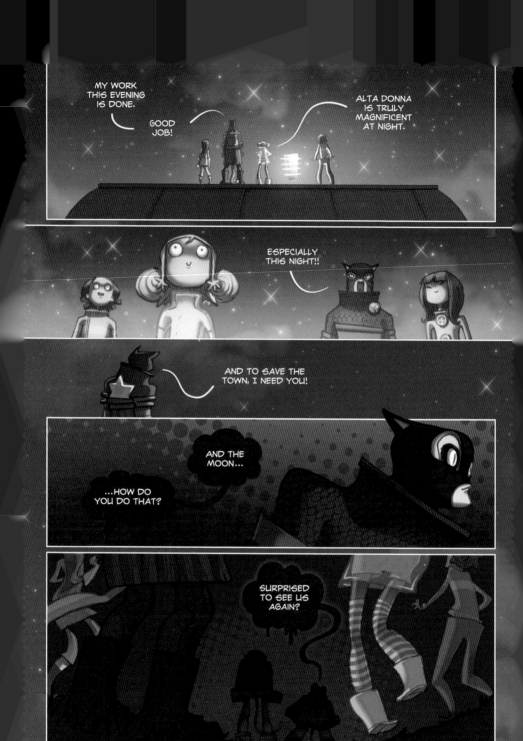

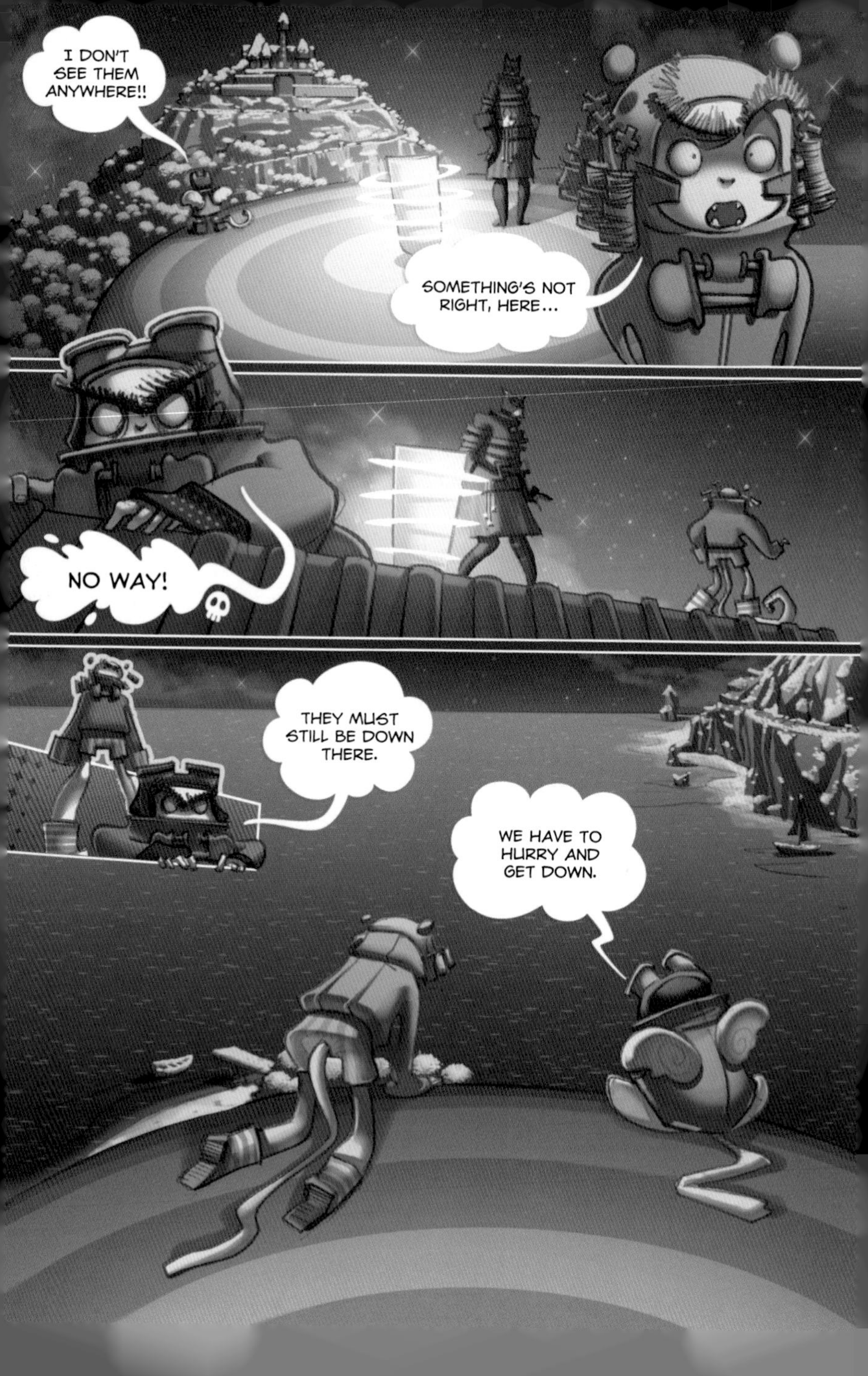

I DON'T SEE THEM ANYWHERE!!
SOMETHING'S NOT RIGHT, HERE...
NO WAY!
THEY MUST STILL BE DOWN THERE.
WE HAVE TO HURRY AND GET DOWN.

WE'RE GOING TO LOSE THEM AGAIN!
WELL, IF WE DO, IT'S NOT MY FAULT!!
THIS IS THE FIRST AND LAST TIME I LISTEN TO YOU!

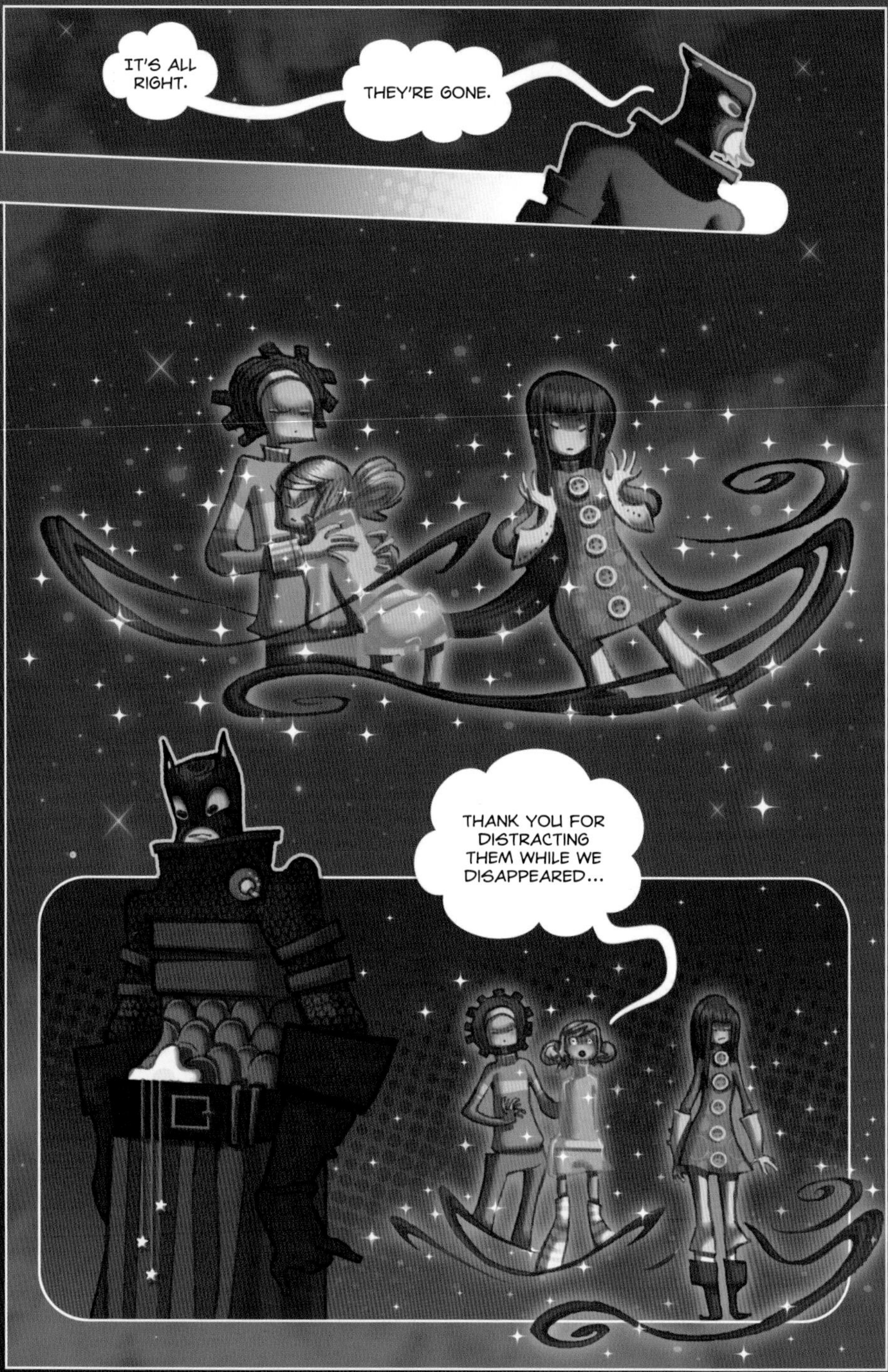
IT'S ALL RIGHT.
THEY'RE GONE.
THANK YOU FOR DISTRACTING THEM WHILE WE DISAPPEARED...

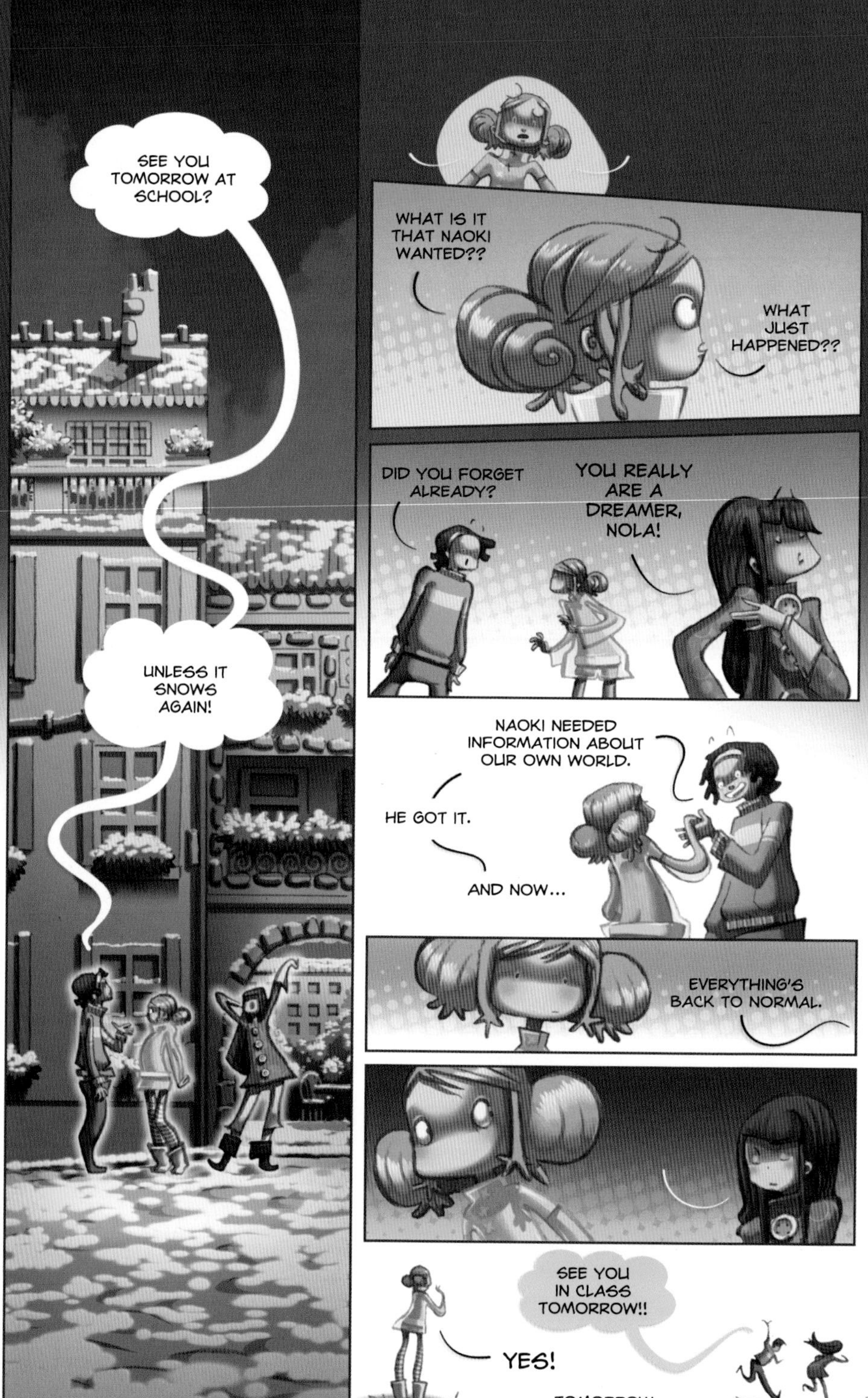
SEE YOU TOMORROW AT SCHOOL?
UNLESS IT SNOWS AGAIN!
WHAT IS IT THAT NAOKI WANTED??
WHAT JUST HAPPENED??
DID YOU FORGET ALREADY?
YOU REALLY ARE A DREAMER, NOLA!
NAOKI NEEDED INFORMATION ABOUT OUR OWN WORLD.
HE GOT IT.
AND NOW...
EVERYTHING'S BACK TO NORMAL.
SEE YOU IN CLASS TOMORROW!!
YES!
...TOMORROW.

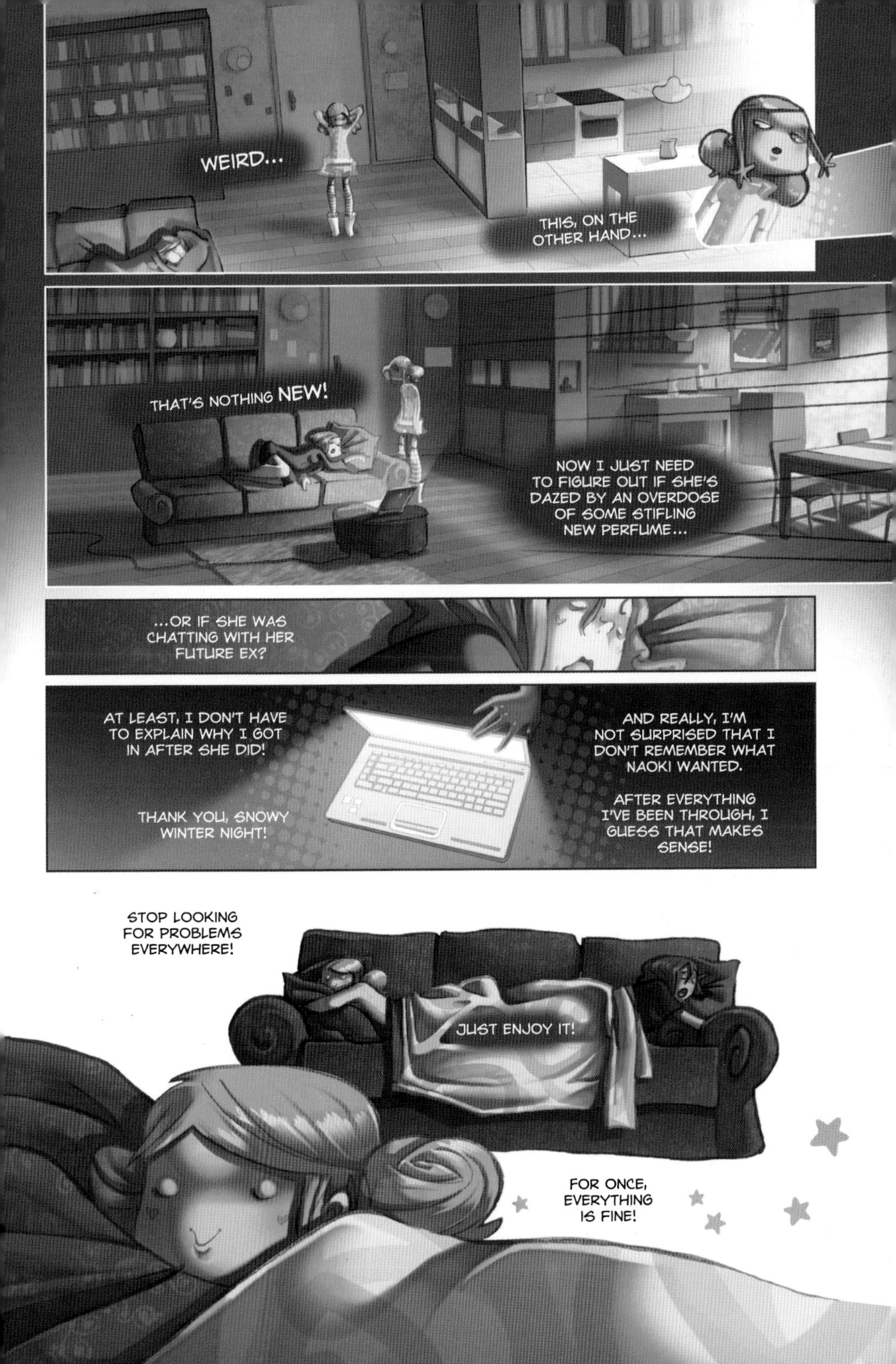
WEIRD...
THIS, ON THE OTHER HAND...
THAT'S NOTHING NEW!
NOW I JUST NEED TO FIGURE OUT IF SHE'S DAZED BY AN OVERDOSE OF SOME STIFLING NEW PERFUME...
...OR IF SHE WAS CHATTING WITH HER FUTURE EX?
AT LEAST, I DON'T HAVE TO EXPLAIN WHY I GOT IN AFTER SHE DID!
THANK YOU, SNOWY WINTER NIGHT!
AND REALLY, I'M NOT SURPRISED THAT I DON'T REMEMBER WHAT NAOKI WANTED.
AFTER EVERYTHING I'VE BEEN THROUGH, I GUESS THAT MAKES SENSE!
STOP LOOKING FOR PROBLEMS EVERYWHERE!
JUST ENJOY IT!
FOR ONCE, EVERYTHING IS FINE!

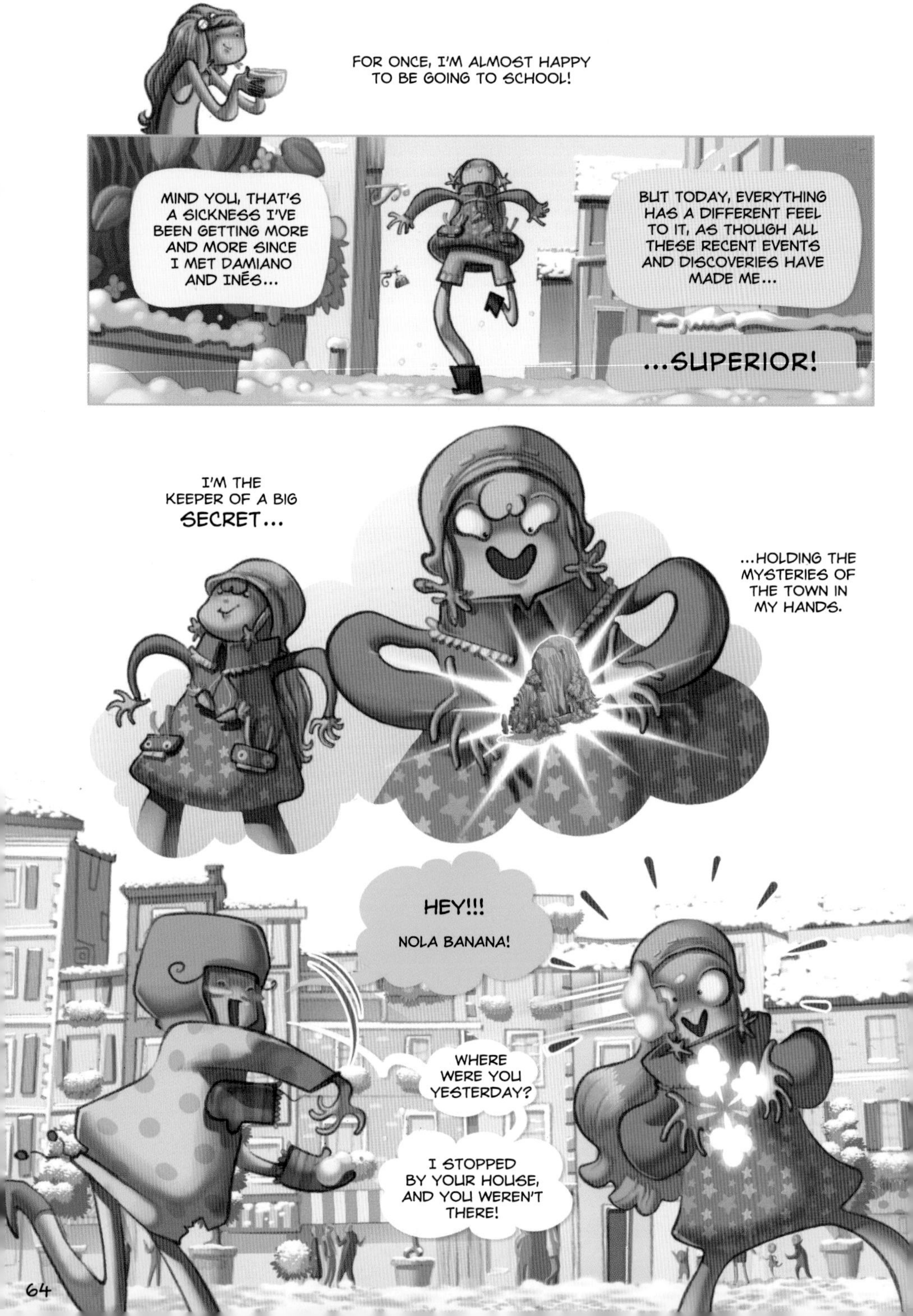
FOR ONCE, I'M ALMOST HAPPY TO BE GOING TO SCHOOL!
MIND YOU, THAT'S A SICKNESS I'VE BEEN GETTING MORE AND MORE SINCE I MET DAMIANO AND INÉS...
BUT TODAY, EVERYTHING HAS A DIFFERENT FEEL TO IT, AS THOUGH ALL THESE RECENT EVENTS AND DISCOVERIES HAVE MADE ME...
...SUPERIOR!
I'M THE KEEPER OF A BIG SECRET...
...HOLDING THE MYSTERIES OF THE TOWN IN MY HANDS.
HEY!!!
NOLA BANANA!
WHERE WERE YOU YESTERDAY?
I STOPPED BY YOUR HOUSE, AND YOU WEREN'T THERE!

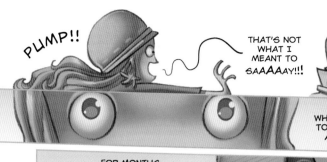

PUMP!!

THAT'S NOT WHAT I MEANT TO SAAAAAY!!!

BUT THAT'S WHAT YOU DID SAY!

WHY DO I NEVER MANAGE TO SAY THE RIGHT THING AT A TIME LIKE THIS?

FOR MONTHS YOU'VE MADE ME FEEL GUILTY ABOUT LEAVING OUR SCHOOL AT THE END OF THE YEAR, WHEN THERE'S NOTHING I CAN DO ABOUT IT.

YOU'RE BLAMING ME FOR LEAVING YOU ALONE...

...BUT YOU'VE ALREADY REPLACED ME...

...AND FORGOTTEN ME.

NOT AT ALL...

YOU'RE MY BEST FRIEND.

AND I DON'T WANT YOU TO GO OFF WITHOUT ME.

THAT'S NORMAL.

SO...I TOLD YOU THAT IT WAS HARD TO KEEP EVERYTHING I'VE DISCOVERED FROM MY BEST FRIEND.

PUMP...

NO...

...YOU ACT LIKE YOU'RE BETTER THAN ME.

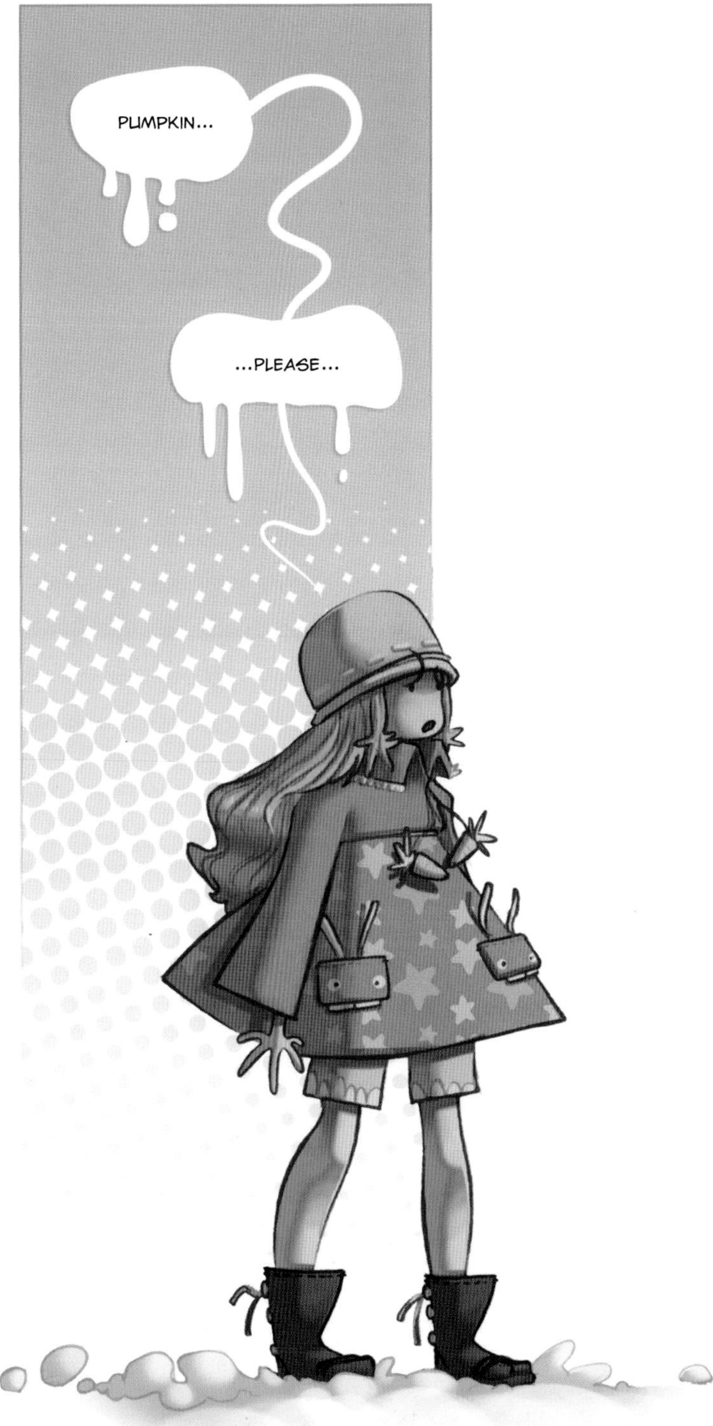
PUMPKIN...
...PLEASE...

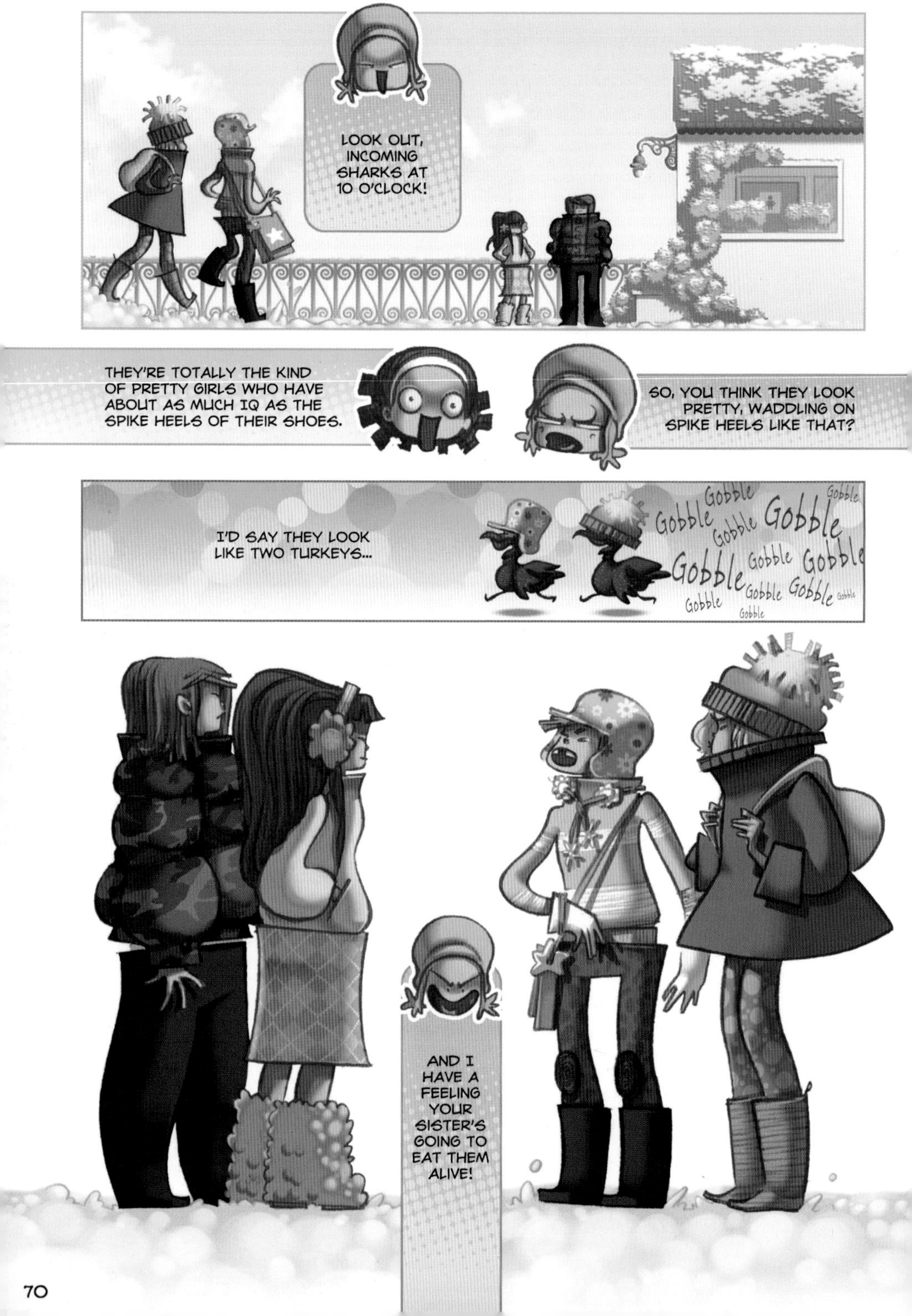

LOOK OUT, INCOMING SHARKS AT 10 O'CLOCK!
THEY'RE TOTALLY THE KIND OF PRETTY GIRLS WHO HAVE ABOUT AS MUCH IQ AS THE SPIKE HEELS OF THEIR SHOES.
SO, YOU THINK THEY LOOK PRETTY, WADDLING ON SPIKE HEELS LIKE THAT?
I'D SAY THEY LOOK LIKE TWO TURKEYS...
Gobble Gobble Gobble Gobble Gobble Gobble Gobble Gobble Gobble Gobble Gobble Gobble
AND I HAVE A FEELING YOUR SISTER'S GOING TO EAT THEM ALIVE!

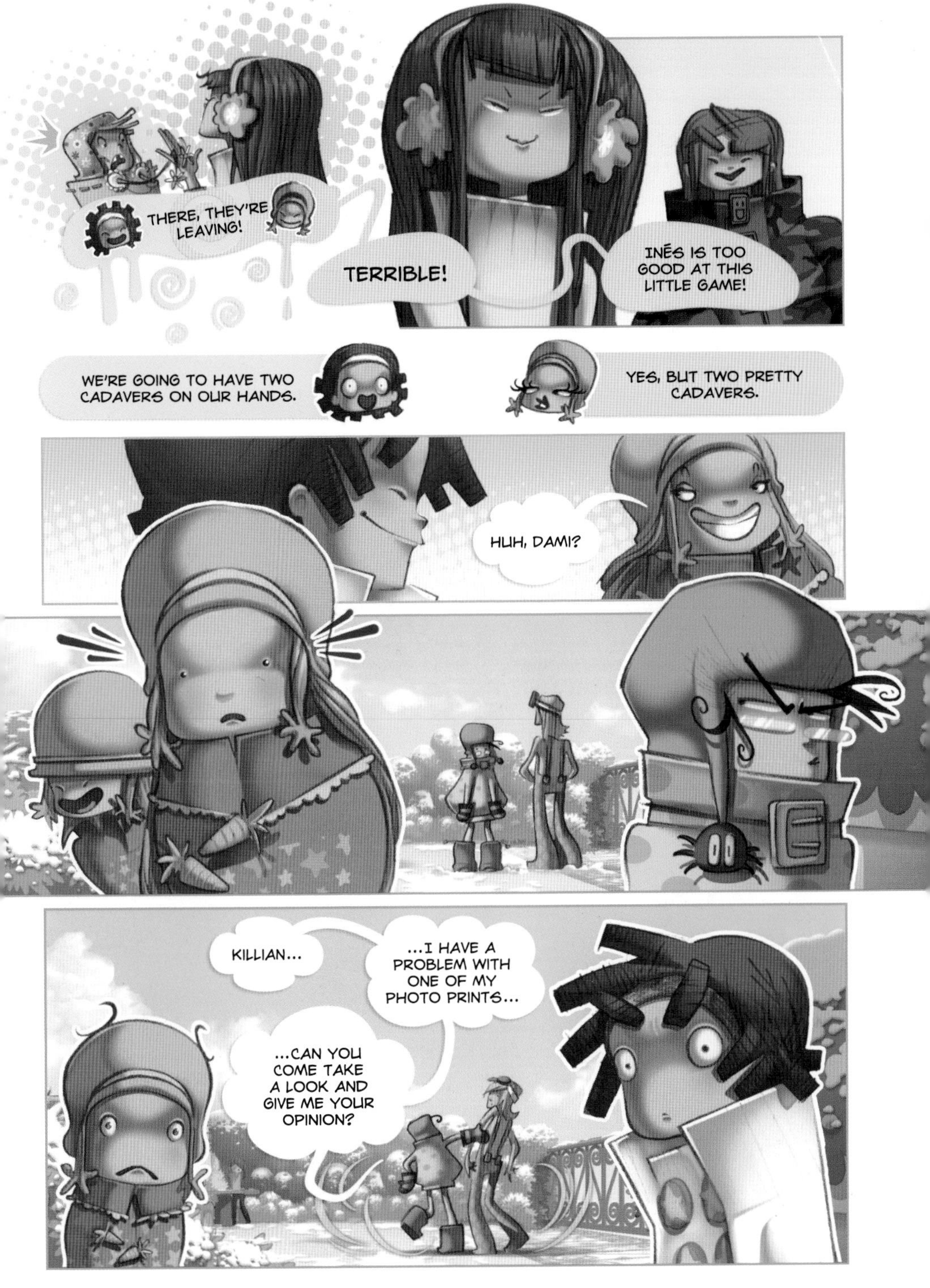

THERE, THEY'RE LEAVING!
TERRIBLE!
INÉS IS TOO GOOD AT THIS LITTLE GAME!
WE'RE GOING TO HAVE TWO CADAVERS ON OUR HANDS.
YES, BUT TWO PRETTY CADAVERS.
HUH, DAMI?
KILLIAN...
...I HAVE A PROBLEM WITH ONE OF MY PHOTO PRINTS...
...CAN YOU COME TAKE A LOOK AND GIVE ME YOUR OPINION?

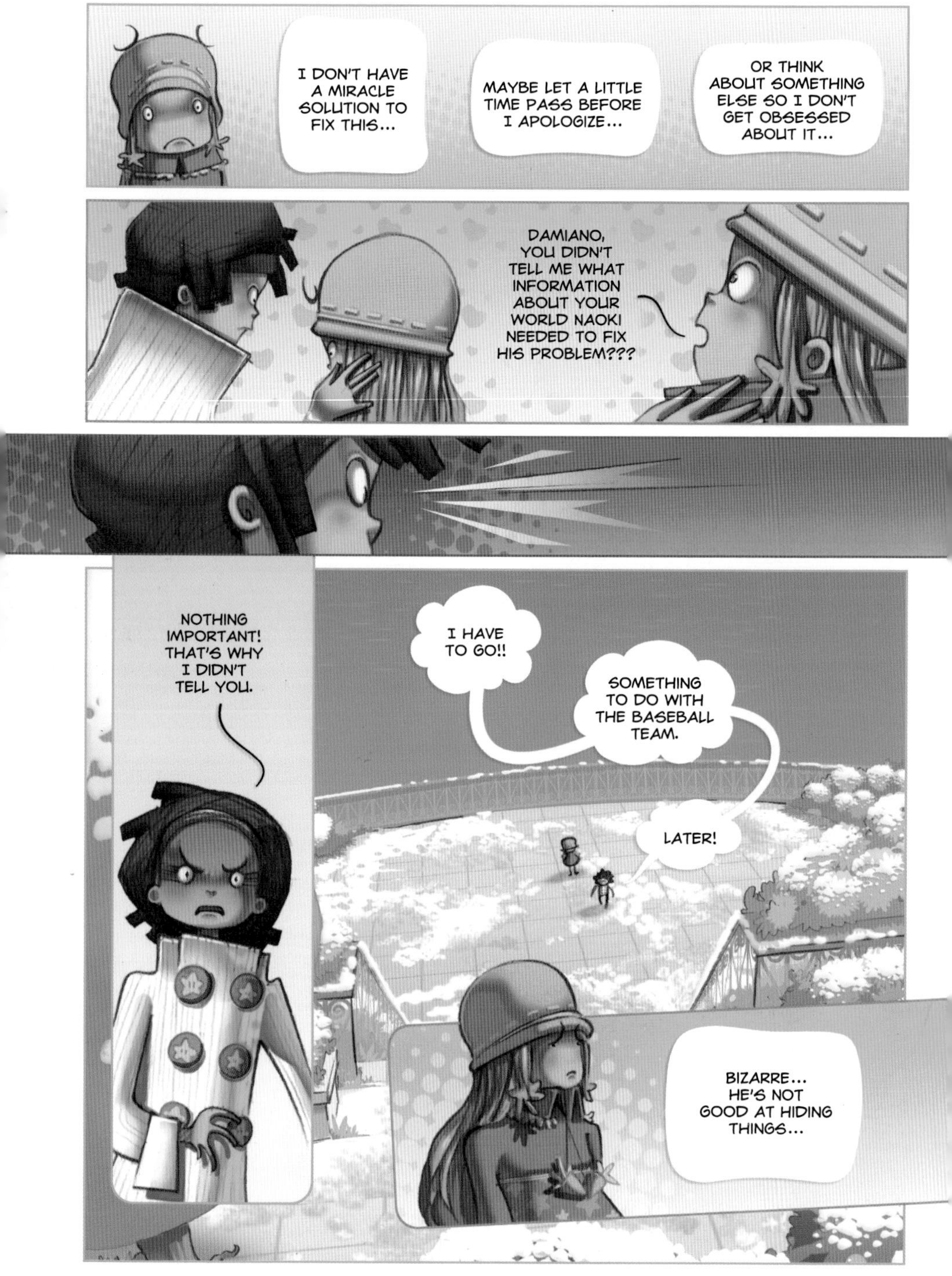

I DON'T HAVE A MIRACLE SOLUTION TO FIX THIS...
MAYBE LET A LITTLE TIME PASS BEFORE I APOLOGIZE...
OR THINK ABOUT SOMETHING ELSE SO I DON'T GET OBSESSED ABOUT IT...
DAMIANO, YOU DIDN'T TELL ME WHAT INFORMATION ABOUT YOUR WORLD NAOKI NEEDED TO FIX HIS PROBLEM???
NOTHING IMPORTANT! THAT'S WHY I DIDN'T TELL YOU.
I HAVE TO GO!!
SOMETHING TO DO WITH THE BASEBALL TEAM.
LATER!
BIZARRE... HE'S NOT GOOD AT HIDING THINGS...

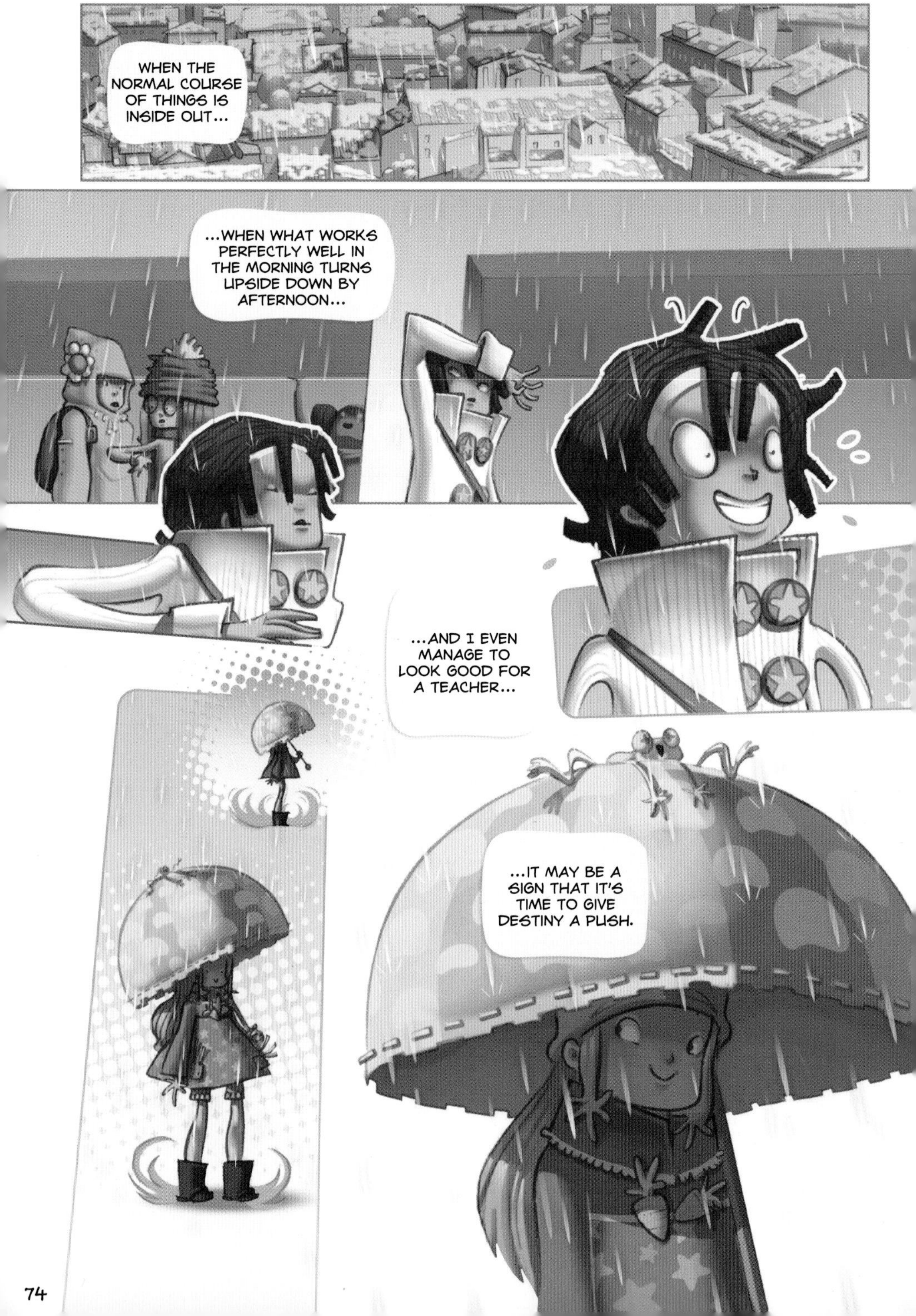
WHEN THE NORMAL COURSE OF THINGS IS INSIDE OUT...
...WHEN WHAT WORKS PERFECTLY WELL IN THE MORNING TURNS UPSIDE DOWN BY AFTERNOON...
...AND I EVEN MANAGE TO LOOK GOOD FOR A TEACHER...
...IT MAY BE A SIGN THAT IT'S TIME TO GIVE DESTINY A PUSH.

76

BY THE WAY...
...WHY'D YOU RUN OFF SO FAST EARLIER?
DOES IT BOTHER YOU IF I TALK ABOUT THE FERRETS???
NO, NO.
MM HMM...
...AND WHEN A QUESTION IS ON THE TIP OF MY TONGUE...
...I CAN'T STOP MYSELF FROM BLURTING IT OUT!!
IF IT'S BECAUSE YOU WERE AFRAID SOMEONE WOULD HEAR US AT SCHOOL...
...THERE NOW...
...WE'RE ALL ALONE!
YOU CAN TELL ME WHAT NAOKI WANTED TO KNOW!
NOTHING!
NAOKI TOLD US WHAT TO DO.
AND WE'LL DO IT!
WHAT DO YOU MEAN, WHAT TO DO?
I THOUGHT HE JUST NEEDED INFO!

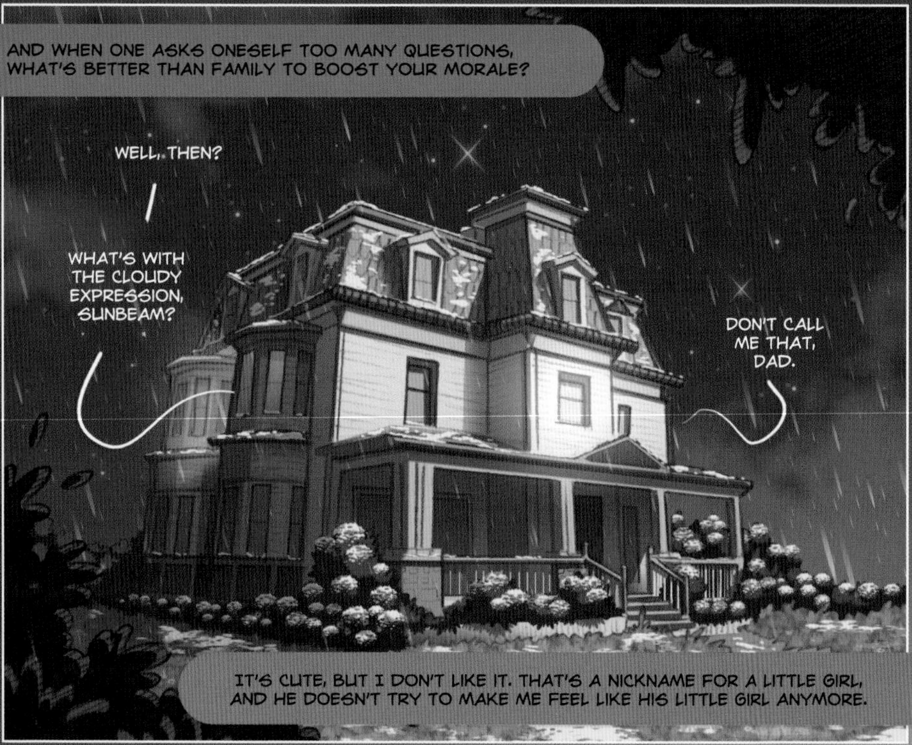
AND WHEN ONE ASKS ONESELF TOO MANY QUESTIONS, WHAT'S BETTER THAN FAMILY TO BOOST YOUR MORALE?
WELL, THEN?
WHAT'S WITH THE CLOUDY EXPRESSION, SUNBEAM?
DON'T CALL ME THAT, DAD.
IT'S CUTE, BUT I DON'T LIKE IT. THAT'S A NICKNAME FOR A LITTLE GIRL, AND HE DOESN'T TRY TO MAKE ME FEEL LIKE HIS LITTLE GIRL ANYMORE.

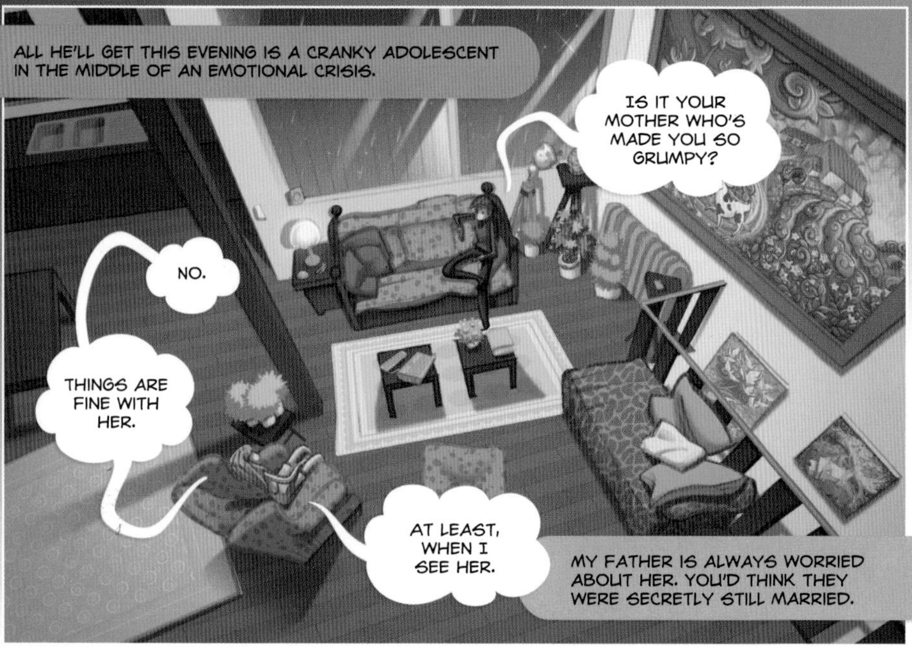
ALL HE'LL GET THIS EVENING IS A CRANKY ADOLESCENT IN THE MIDDLE OF AN EMOTIONAL CRISIS.
IS IT YOUR MOTHER WHO'S MADE YOU SO GRUMPY?
NO.
THINGS ARE FINE WITH HER.
AT LEAST, WHEN I SEE HER.
MY FATHER IS ALWAYS WORRIED ABOUT HER. YOU'D THINK THEY WERE SECRETLY STILL MARRIED.

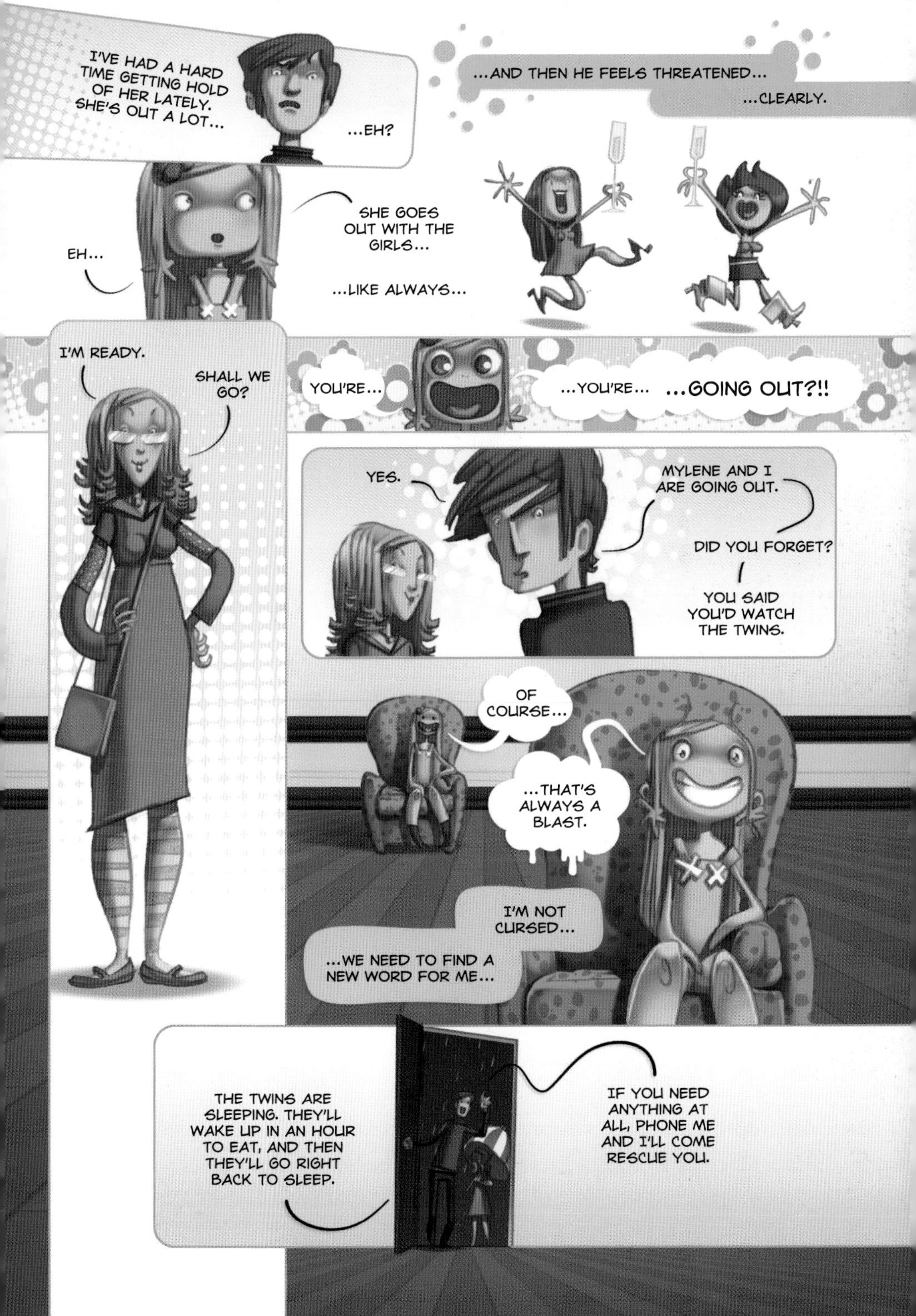
I'VE HAD A HARD TIME GETTING HOLD OF HER LATELY. SHE'S OUT A LOT...
...EH?
...AND THEN HE FEELS THREATENED...
...CLEARLY.
EH...
SHE GOES OUT WITH THE GIRLS...
...LIKE ALWAYS...
I'M READY.
SHALL WE GO?
YOU'RE...
...YOU'RE...
...GOING OUT?!!
YES.
MYLENE AND I ARE GOING OUT.
DID YOU FORGET?
YOU SAID YOU'D WATCH THE TWINS.
OF COURSE...
...THAT'S ALWAYS A BLAST.
I'M NOT CURSED...
...WE NEED TO FIND A NEW WORD FOR ME...
THE TWINS ARE SLEEPING. THEY'LL WAKE UP IN AN HOUR TO EAT, AND THEN THEY'LL GO RIGHT BACK TO SLEEP.
IF YOU NEED ANYTHING AT ALL, PHONE ME AND I'LL COME RESCUE YOU.

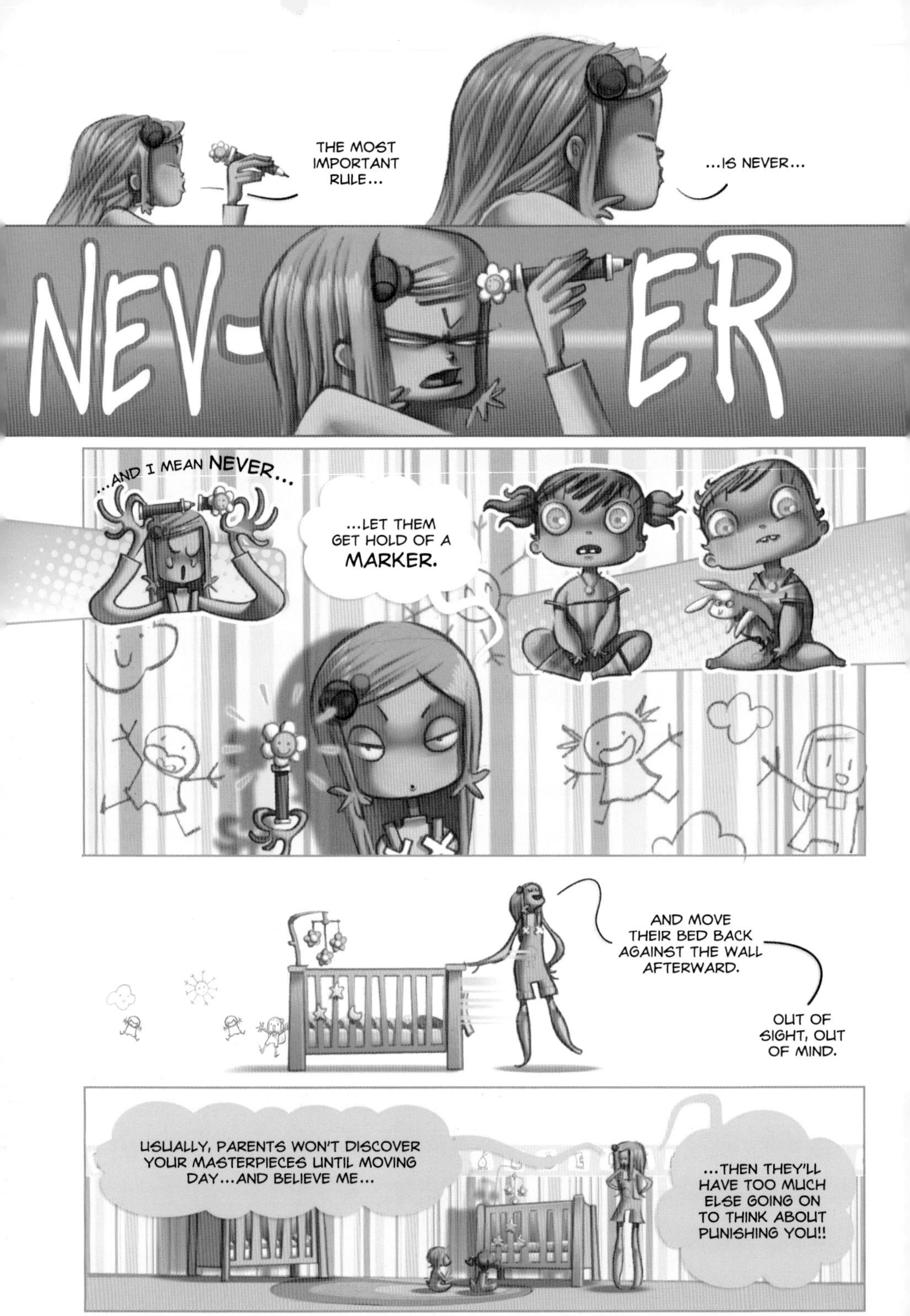
THE MOST IMPORTANT RULE...
...IS NEVER...
NEV-ER
...AND I MEAN NEVER...
...LET THEM GET HOLD OF A MARKER.
AND MOVE THEIR BED BACK AGAINST THE WALL AFTERWARD.
OUT OF SIGHT, OUT OF MIND.
USUALLY, PARENTS WON'T DISCOVER YOUR MASTERPIECES UNTIL MOVING DAY...AND BELIEVE ME...
...THEN THEY'LL HAVE TOO MUCH ELSE GOING ON TO THINK ABOUT PUNISHING YOU!!

EVERYTHING WENT WELL?

JUST LIKE YOU SAID!

IT WAS SUPER CALM AND EASY!

THE SMALL FRIES ARE ASLEEP...

...I'LL GET GOING.

WAIT!

HAVE SOME FUN WITH THIS.

I HAVE SOMETHING FOR YOU.

SPEND IT ON SOME CLOTHES AND MUSIC.

THANKS FOR THIS SUPER-CHEERING-UP EVENING, DAD.

YOU ALWAYS KNOW JUST WHAT TO DO.

EVEN YOUR WIFE IS SUPER ANNOYING.

SHE'S ALWAYS TOO NICE, AND I CAN'T EVEN WORK UP THE ENERGY TO DISLIKE HER...

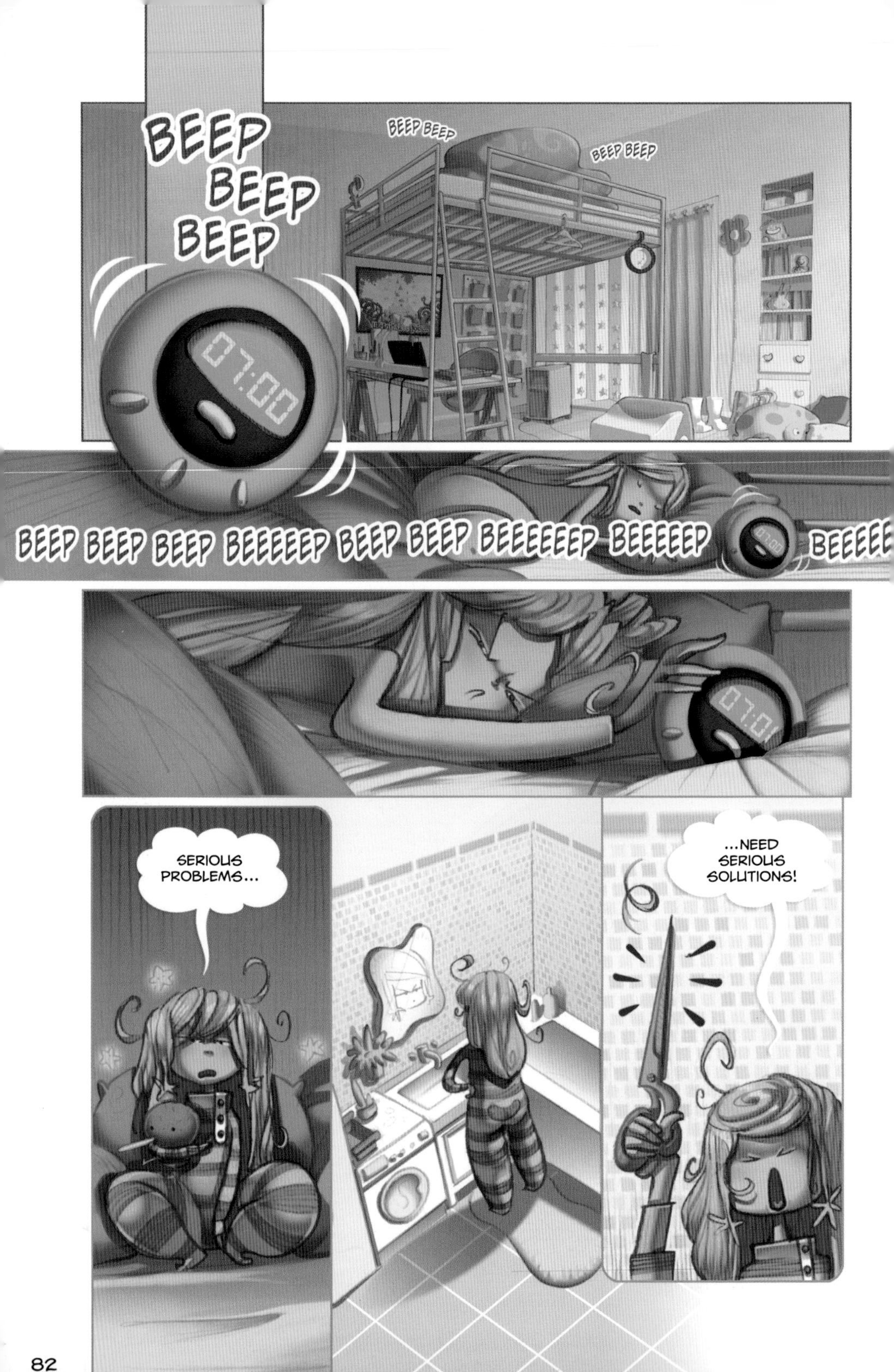
BEEP BEEP BEEP
BEEP BEEP
BEEP BEEP
BEEP BEEP BEEP BEEEEEP BEEP BEEP BEEEEEEP BEEEEEP BEEEEE
SERIOUS PROBLEMS...
...NEED SERIOUS SOLUTIONS!

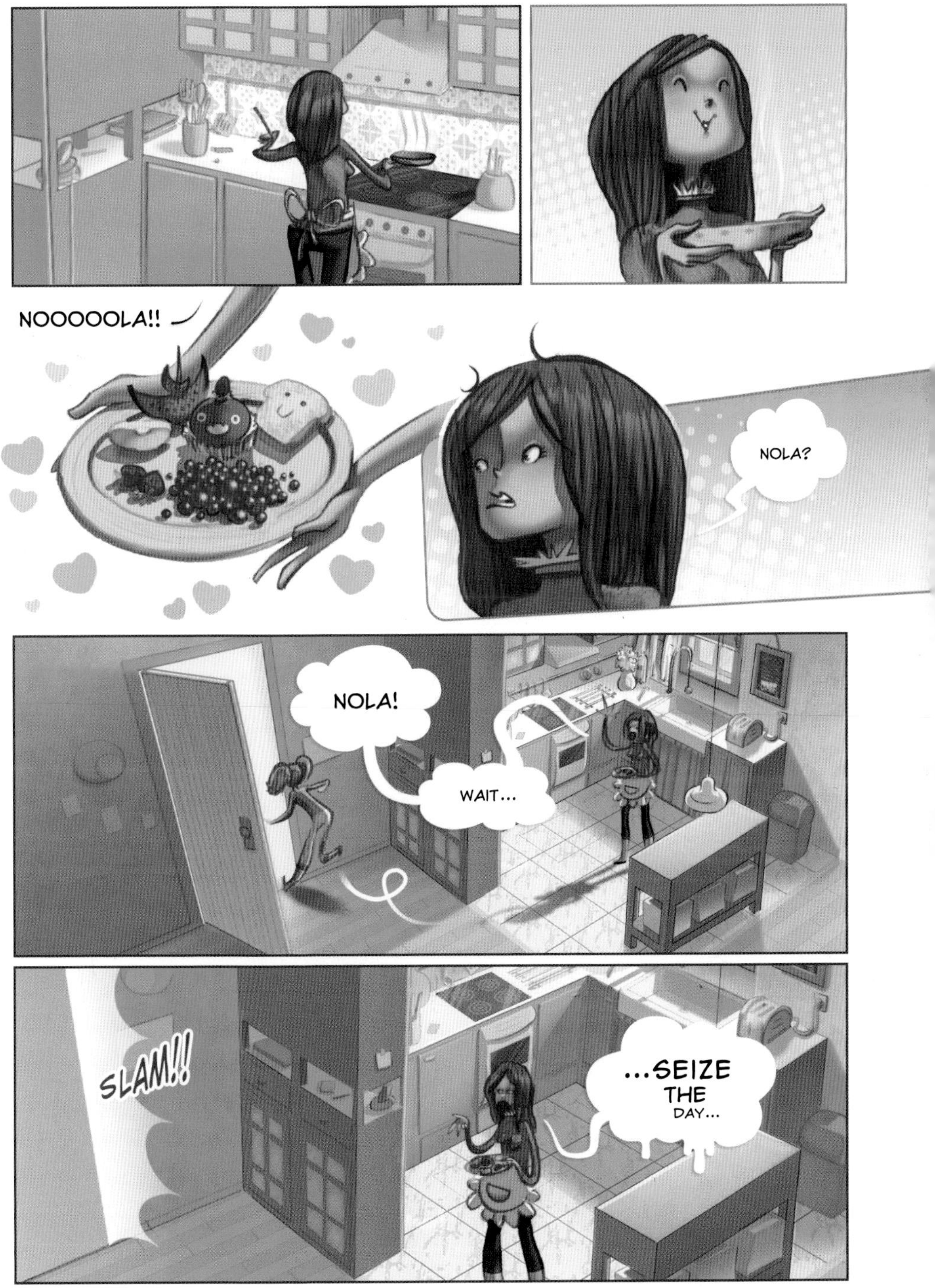
NOOOOOLA!!
NOLA?
NOLA!
WAIT...
SLAM!!
...SEIZE THE DAY...

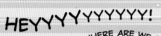

THIS IS NOT YOGA.

THIS IS HOW I WAKE UP.

I NEED SUNLIGHT!

YOU TWO ARE HIDING SOMETHING FROM ME!

I KNOW IT!!

STOP TREATING ME LIKE AN AIRHEAD.

WHATEVER IT IS, I WANT TO KNOW. AND I'LL FIND OUT, NO MATTER WHAT IT TAKES!

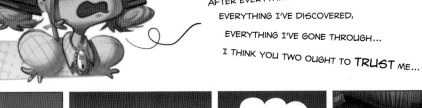

AFTER EVERYTHING I'VE SEEN,

EVERYTHING I'VE DISCOVERED,

EVERYTHING I'VE GONE THROUGH...

I THINK YOU TWO OUGHT TO **TRUST** ME...

WE HAVE NOTHING TO TELL YOU...

...FOR...

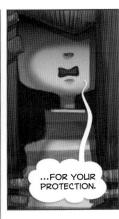

...FOR YOUR PROTECTION.

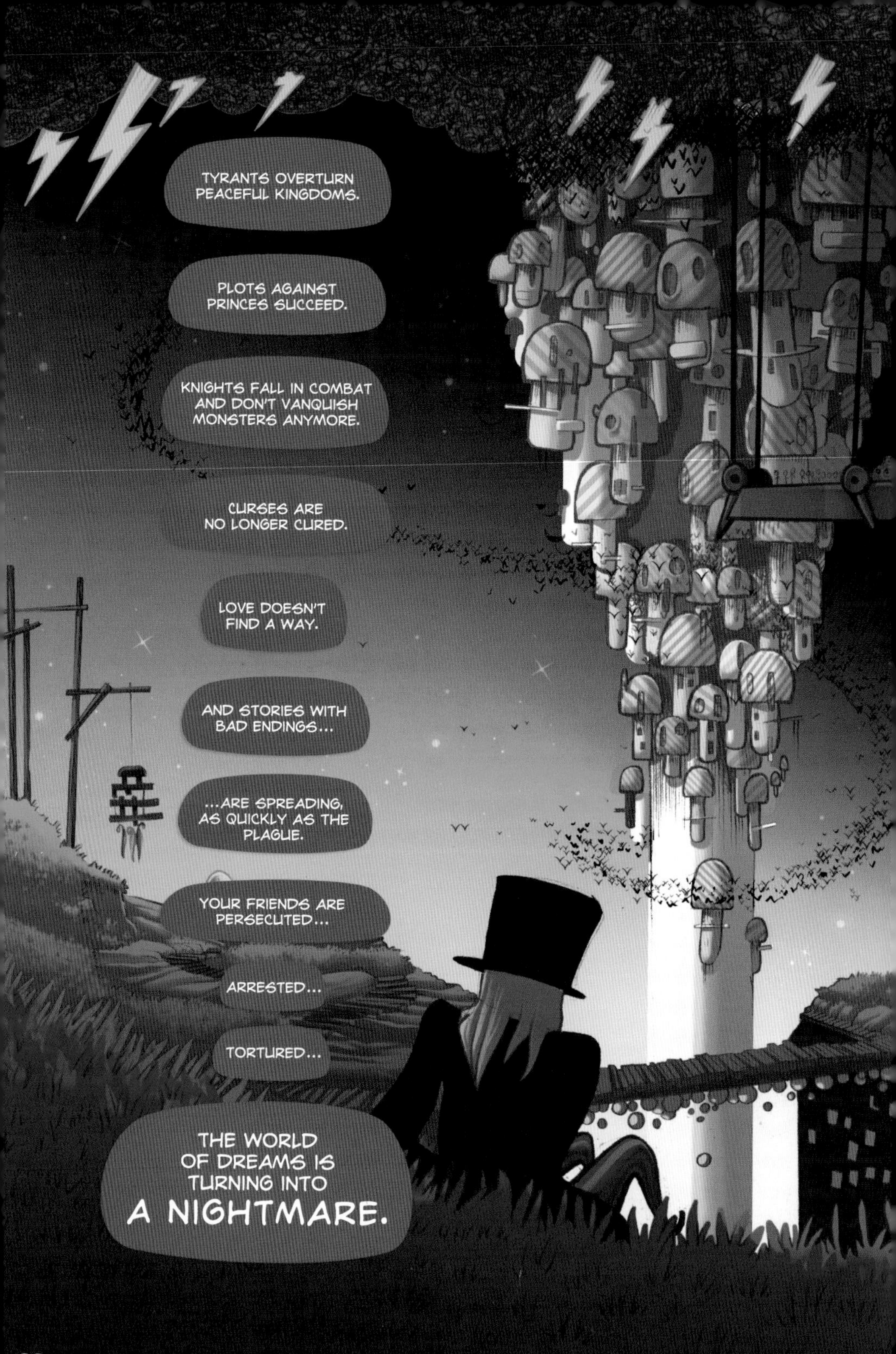
TYRANTS OVERTURN PEACEFUL KINGDOMS.
PLOTS AGAINST PRINCES SUCCEED.
KNIGHTS FALL IN COMBAT AND DON'T VANQUISH MONSTERS ANYMORE.
CURSES ARE NO LONGER CURED.
LOVE DOESN'T FIND A WAY.
AND STORIES WITH BAD ENDINGS...
...ARE SPREADING, AS QUICKLY AS THE PLAGUE.
YOUR FRIENDS ARE PERSECUTED...
ARRESTED...
TORTURED...
THE WORLD OF DREAMS IS TURNING INTO A NIGHTMARE.

AND THESE CHANGES ALSO AFFECT ALTA DONNA.
OUR BEAUTIFUL MECHANISM IS BREAKING DOWN...
...BIT BY BIT...
...AND THE ENTIRE TOWN COULD DISAPPEAR.
WHAT CAN WE DO?
YES, THERE MUST BE SOMETHING WE CAN DO!
A WAY TO REPAIR THE DAMAGE!

IT'S VITAL THAT THE PROPER BALANCE IS RESTORED TO THIS WORLD...

THE STORIES IN YOUR WORLD REPEAT THEMSELVES.

INFINITELY...

...IN A LOOP.

IF EQUILIBRIUM IS RESTORED...

...LITTLE BY LITTLE, THE STORIES WILL RESUME THEIR NORMAL COURSE.

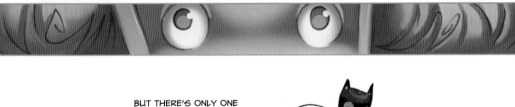

BUT THERE'S ONLY ONE WAY TO REESTABLISH EQUILIBRIUM.

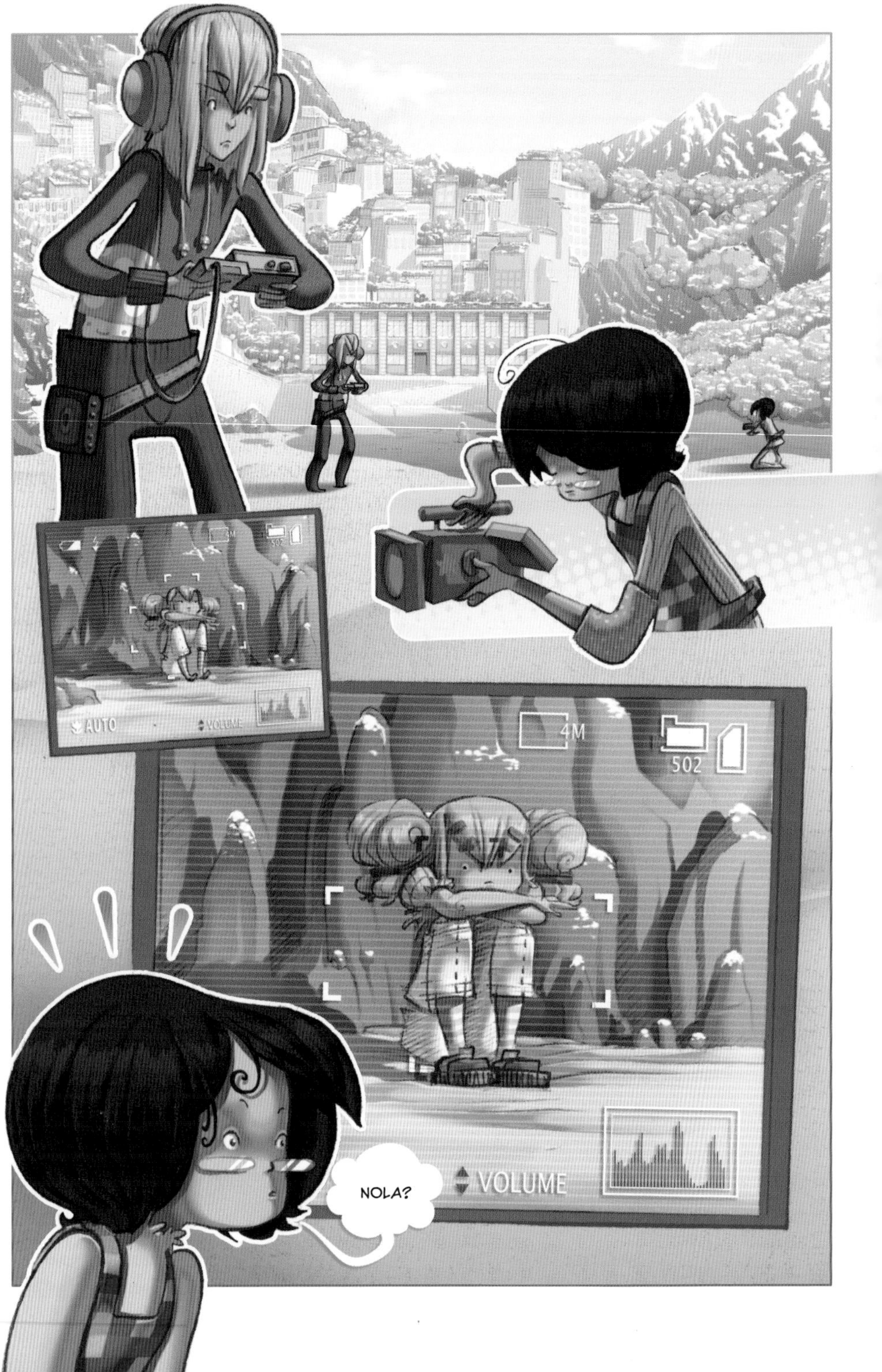

4M
502
AUTO
VOLUME
4M
502
NOLA?
VOLUME

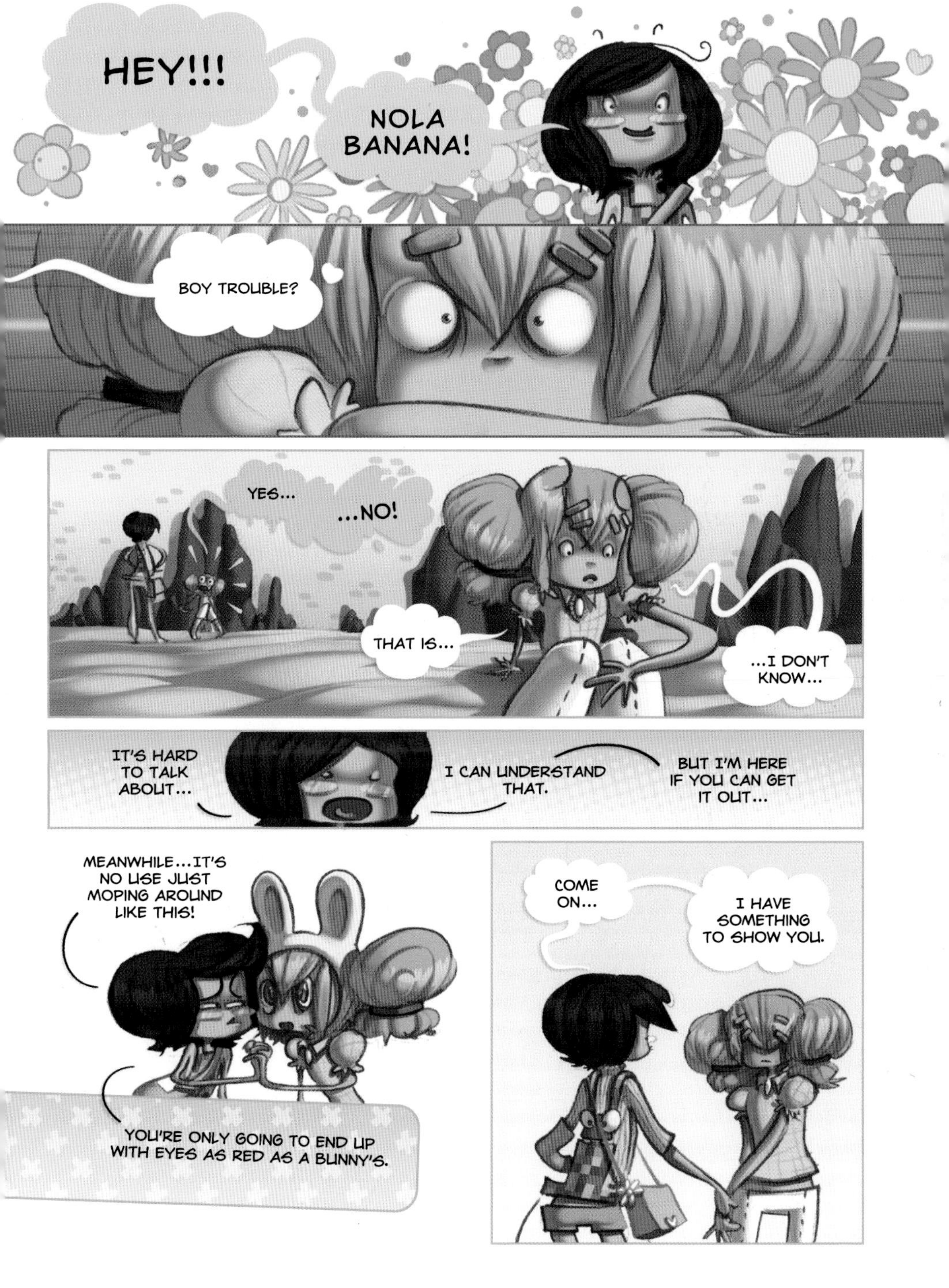
HEY!!!
NOLA BANANA!
BOY TROUBLE?
YES...
...NO!
THAT IS...
...I DON'T KNOW...
IT'S HARD TO TALK ABOUT...
I CAN UNDERSTAND THAT.
BUT I'M HERE IF YOU CAN GET IT OUT...
MEANWHILE...IT'S NO USE JUST MOPING AROUND LIKE THIS!
YOU'RE ONLY GOING TO END UP WITH EYES AS RED AS A BUNNY'S.
COME ON...
I HAVE SOMETHING TO SHOW YOU.

NO DENYING IT: HE'S MORE LIKE ME THAN I WOULD HAVE IMAGINED.

AND LISTENING TO HIM RAMBLE AND BABBLE LIKE A NOLA...

I COULD SEE MY OWN FUTURE...

...WITHOUT DAMIANO AND INÉS.

AS IF AT THE CROSSROADS OF TWO PATHS...

...OF TWO DIFFERENT WORLDS...

ONE OF WHICH I KNEW WELL ENOUGH...

...BUT IN WHICH AMAZING CONNECTIONS COULD GROW.

...TO WANDER WITHOUT A GUIDE, LOST IN MY DREAMS...

AND ANOTHER ONE, MORE DANGEROUS, FULL OF SURPRISES, OF DISCOVERIES, OF POETRY, OF ODD ENCOUNTERS...

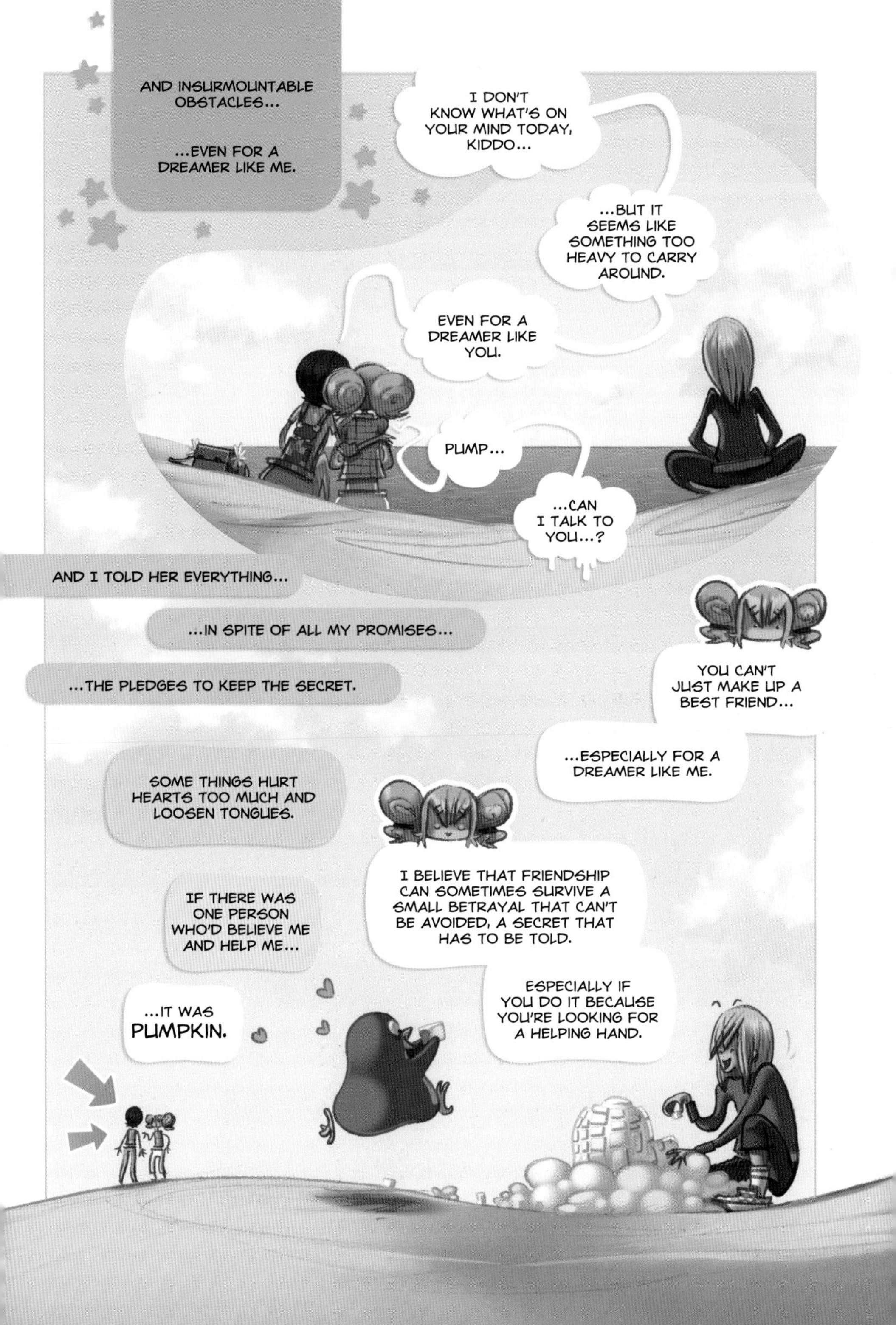
AND INSURMOUNTABLE OBSTACLES...
...EVEN FOR A DREAMER LIKE ME.
I DON'T KNOW WHAT'S ON YOUR MIND TODAY, KIDDO...
...BUT IT SEEMS LIKE SOMETHING TOO HEAVY TO CARRY AROUND.
EVEN FOR A DREAMER LIKE YOU.
PUMP...
...CAN I TALK TO YOU...?
AND I TOLD HER EVERYTHING...
...IN SPITE OF ALL MY PROMISES...
...THE PLEDGES TO KEEP THE SECRET.
YOU CAN'T JUST MAKE UP A BEST FRIEND...
...ESPECIALLY FOR A DREAMER LIKE ME.
SOME THINGS HURT HEARTS TOO MUCH AND LOOSEN TONGUES.
I BELIEVE THAT FRIENDSHIP CAN SOMETIMES SURVIVE A SMALL BETRAYAL THAT CAN'T BE AVOIDED, A SECRET THAT HAS TO BE TOLD.
IF THERE WAS ONE PERSON WHO'D BELIEVE ME AND HELP ME...
ESPECIALLY IF YOU DO IT BECAUSE YOU'RE LOOKING FOR A HELPING HAND.
...IT WAS PUMPKIN.

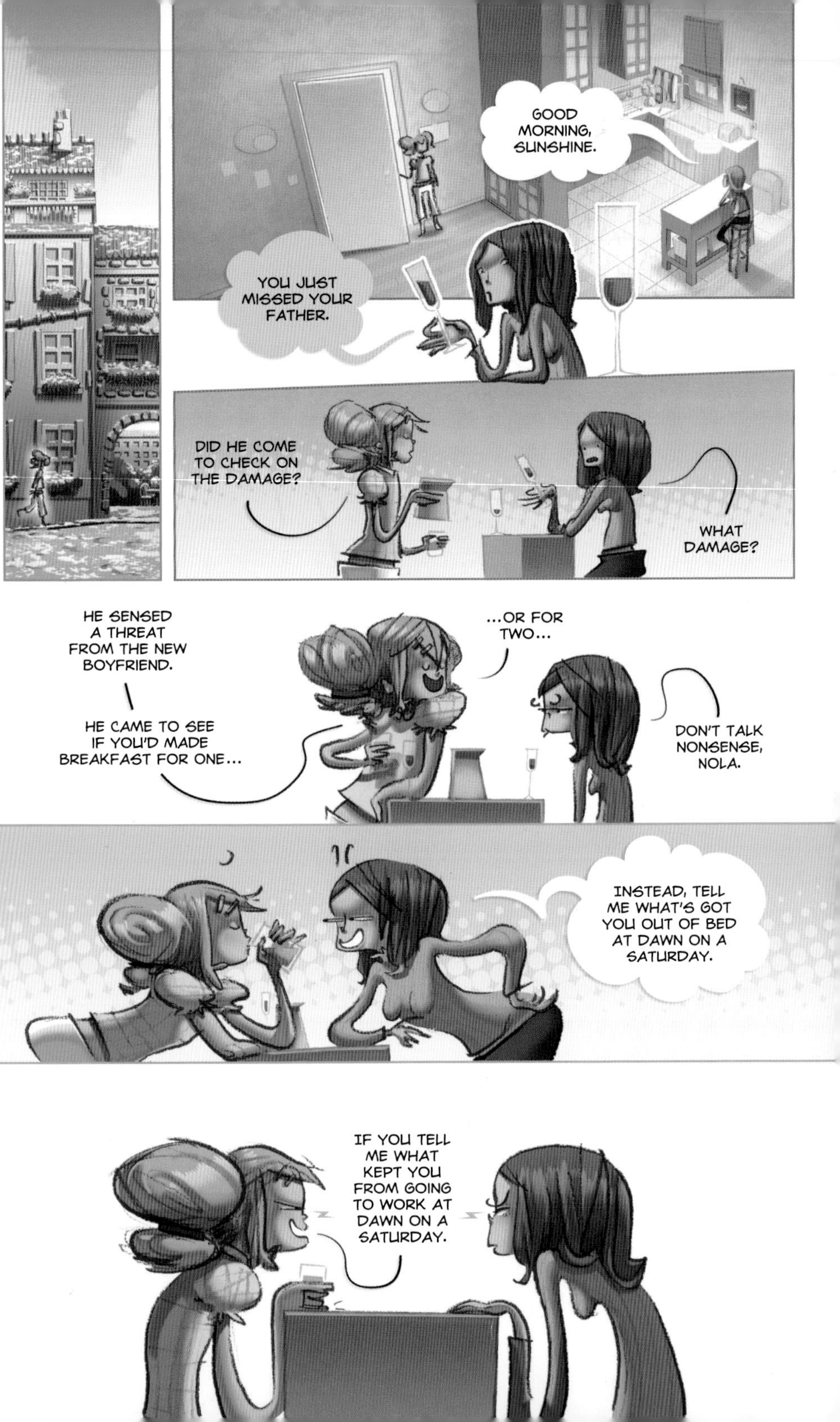
GOOD MORNING, SUNSHINE.
YOU JUST MISSED YOUR FATHER.
DID HE COME TO CHECK ON THE DAMAGE?
WHAT DAMAGE?
HE SENSED A THREAT FROM THE NEW BOYFRIEND.
HE CAME TO SEE IF YOU'D MADE BREAKFAST FOR ONE...
...OR FOR TWO...
DON'T TALK NONSENSE, NOLA.
INSTEAD, TELL ME WHAT'S GOT YOU OUT OF BED AT DAWN ON A SATURDAY.
IF YOU TELL ME WHAT KEPT YOU FROM GOING TO WORK AT DAWN ON A SATURDAY.

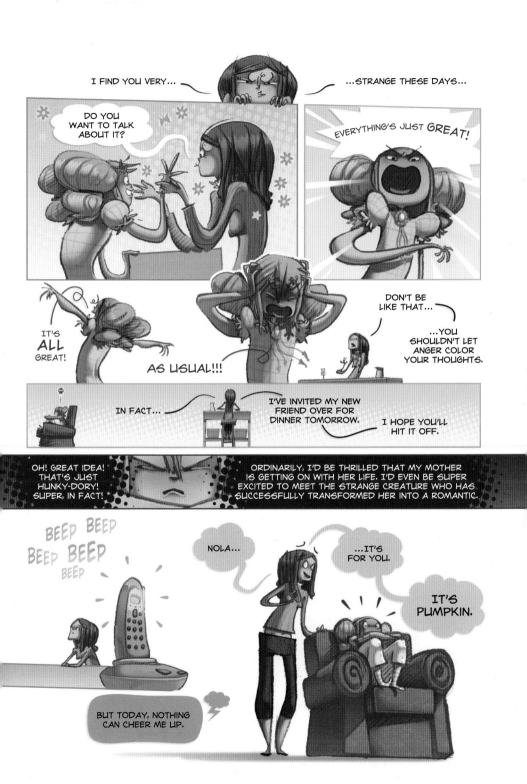

CLEARLY, IT COULDN'T HAVE BEEN DAMIANO AND INÉS...

I DON'T SEE WHY YOUR GIANT FERRET WOULD HAVE DONE IT, EITHER.

TAP! TAP! TAP!

IN STORIES, THEY ALWAYS HAVE TO GO BACK TO THE BEGINNING TO SOLVE THE MYSTERY.

I'M SURE THE LIBRARIAN HAS AN ANSWER FOR ALL THIS!

HOW DO YOU KNOW ALL THIS?

AN OVERDOSE OF DETECTIVE NOVELS!

I EVEN STARTED MY OWN PRIVATE INVESTIGATION CLUB WHEN I STARTED AT OUR SCHOOL. BUT THERE ARE NEVER ANY CRIMES IN THIS TOWN...

THIS IS WHY PUMPKIN IS THE BEST!

SHE'S THE ONLY ONE WHO CAN COME UP WITH CRAZIER, MORE RIDICULOUS IDEAS THAN I DO!

WHY?!

THE PASSAGE...

...THE IN-BETWEEN WORLD.

WHY HASN'T HE COME BACK?

NEED HIM!!

WHERE'S THE CAT?

WELL...

...LET'S GET STARTED.

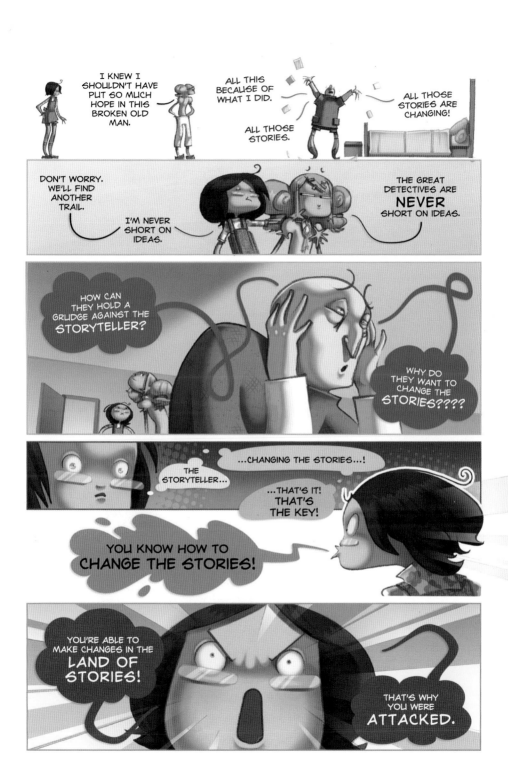

NOLA!

I KNOW HOW TO FIX EVERYTHING SO DAMIANO AND INÉS DON'T HAVE TO LEAVE.

HOW???

THIS IS VERY IMPORTANT!

TELL US HOW TO CHANGE THE STORIES!

LUCKILY, PUMPKIN KNOWS HOW TO CROSS-EXAMINE A WITNESS!

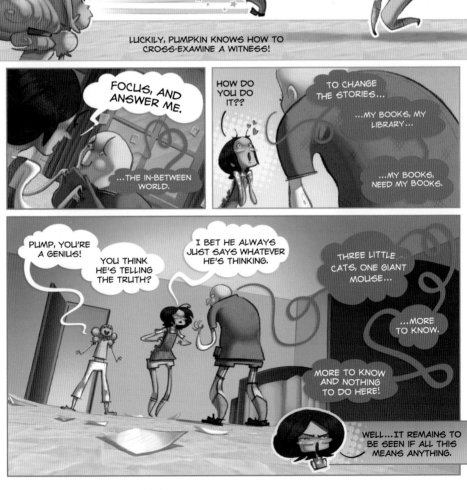

FOCUS, AND ANSWER ME.

...THE IN-BETWEEN WORLD.

HOW DO YOU DO IT??

TO CHANGE THE STORIES...

...MY BOOKS, MY LIBRARY...

...MY BOOKS, NEED MY BOOKS.

PUMP, YOU'RE A GENIUS!

YOU THINK HE'S TELLING THE TRUTH?

I BET HE ALWAYS JUST SAYS WHATEVER HE'S THINKING.

THREE LITTLE CATS, ONE GIANT MOUSE...

...MORE TO KNOW.

MORE TO KNOW AND NOTHING TO DO HERE!

WELL...IT REMAINS TO BE SEEN IF ALL THIS MEANS ANYTHING.

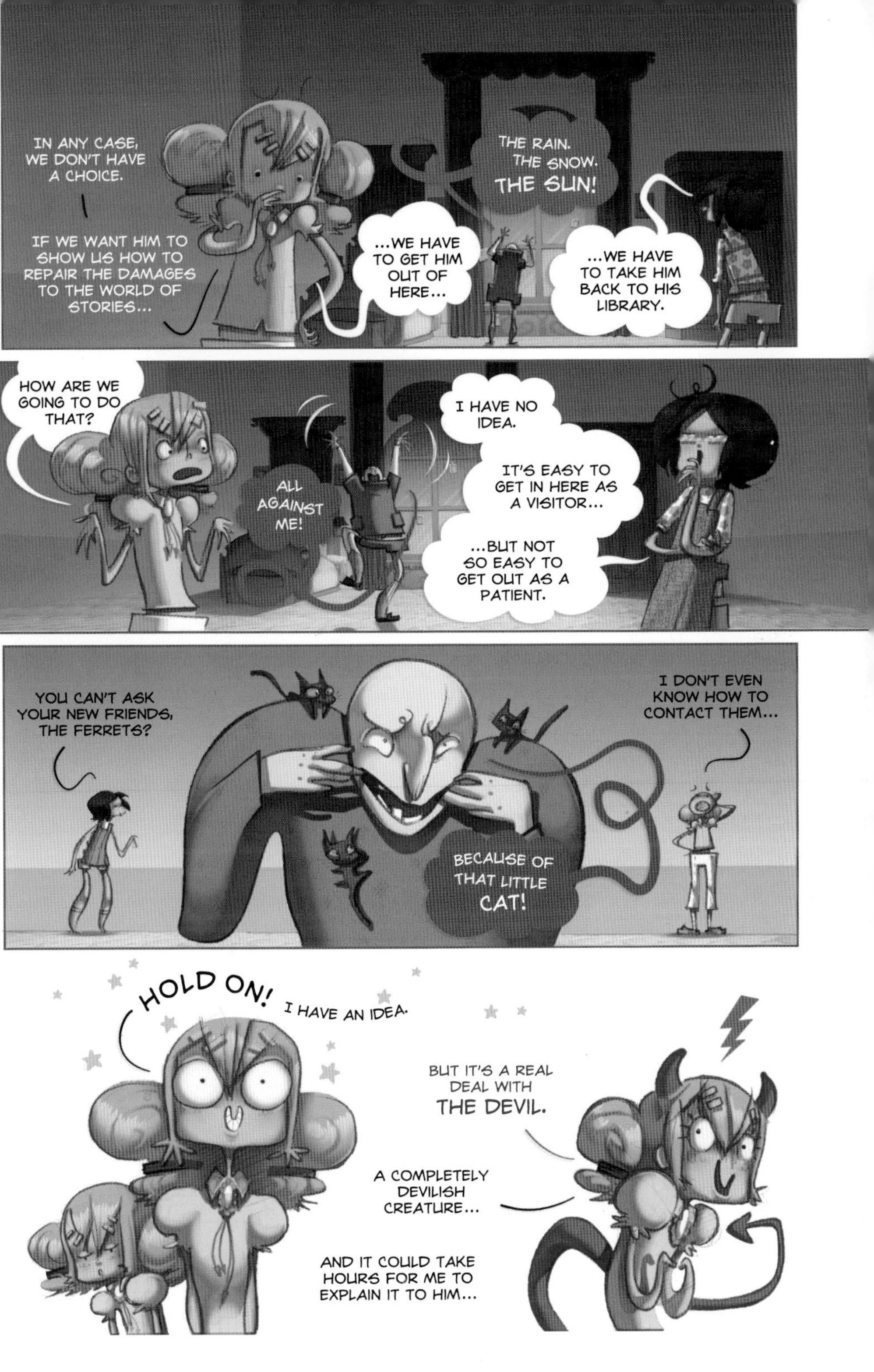
IN ANY CASE, WE DON'T HAVE A CHOICE.
IF WE WANT HIM TO SHOW US HOW TO REPAIR THE DAMAGES TO THE WORLD OF STORIES...
...WE HAVE TO GET HIM OUT OF HERE...
THE RAIN. THE SNOW. THE SUN!
...WE HAVE TO TAKE HIM BACK TO HIS LIBRARY.
HOW ARE WE GOING TO DO THAT?
ALL AGAINST ME!
I HAVE NO IDEA.
IT'S EASY TO GET IN HERE AS A VISITOR...
...BUT NOT SO EASY TO GET OUT AS A PATIENT.
YOU CAN'T ASK YOUR NEW FRIENDS, THE FERRETS?
BECAUSE OF THAT LITTLE CAT!
I DON'T EVEN KNOW HOW TO CONTACT THEM...
HOLD ON! I HAVE AN IDEA.
BUT IT'S A REAL DEAL WITH THE DEVIL.
A COMPLETELY DEVILISH CREATURE...
AND IT COULD TAKE HOURS FOR ME TO EXPLAIN IT TO HIM...

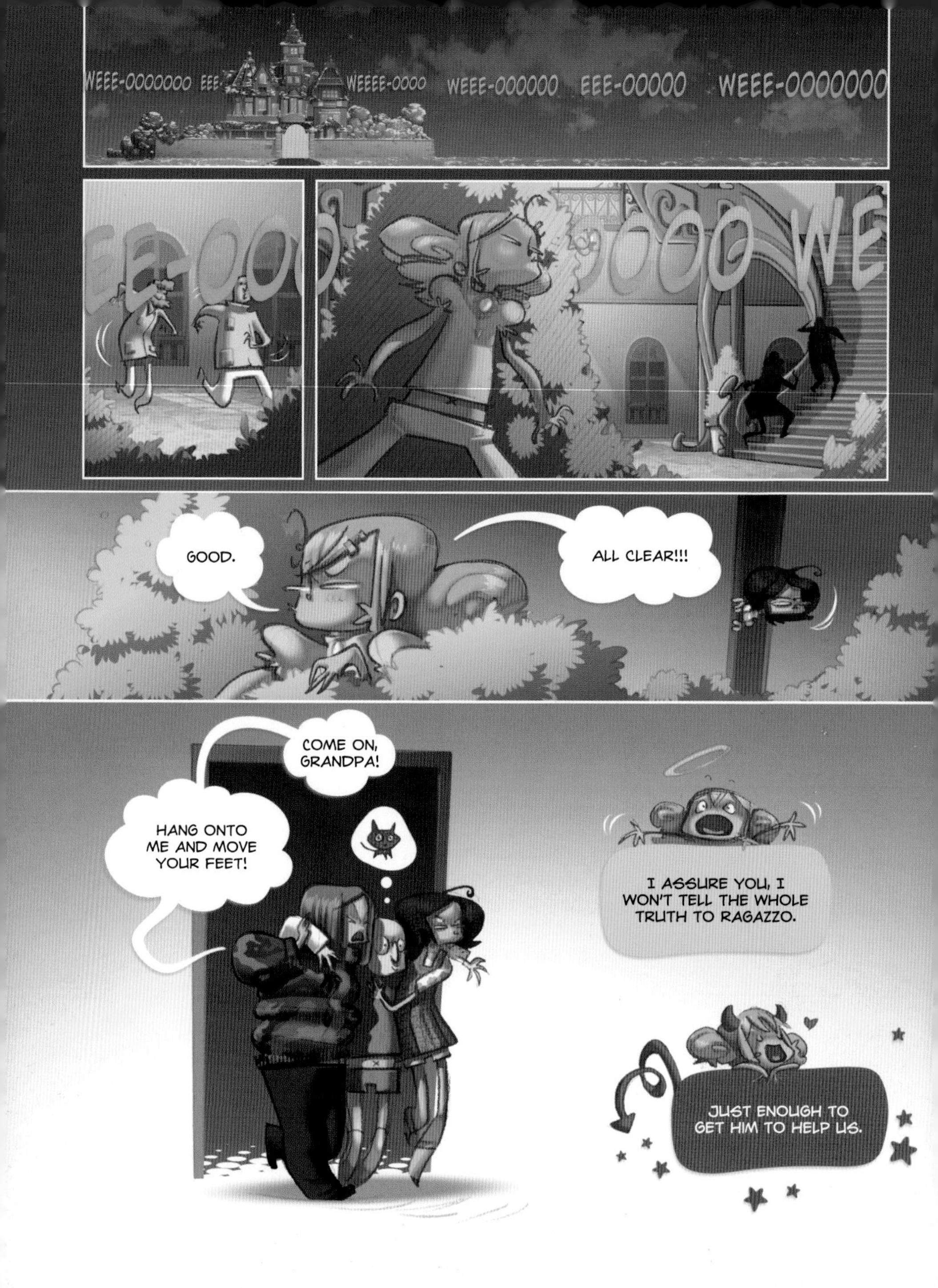
WEEE-OOOOOOO EEE-
WEEEE-OOOO
WEEE-OOOOOO
EEE-OOOOO
WEEE-OOOOOOO
GOOD.
ALL CLEAR!!!
COME ON, GRANDPA!
HANG ONTO ME AND MOVE YOUR FEET!
I ASSURE YOU, I WON'T TELL THE WHOLE TRUTH TO RAGAZZO.
JUST ENOUGH TO GET HIM TO HELP US.

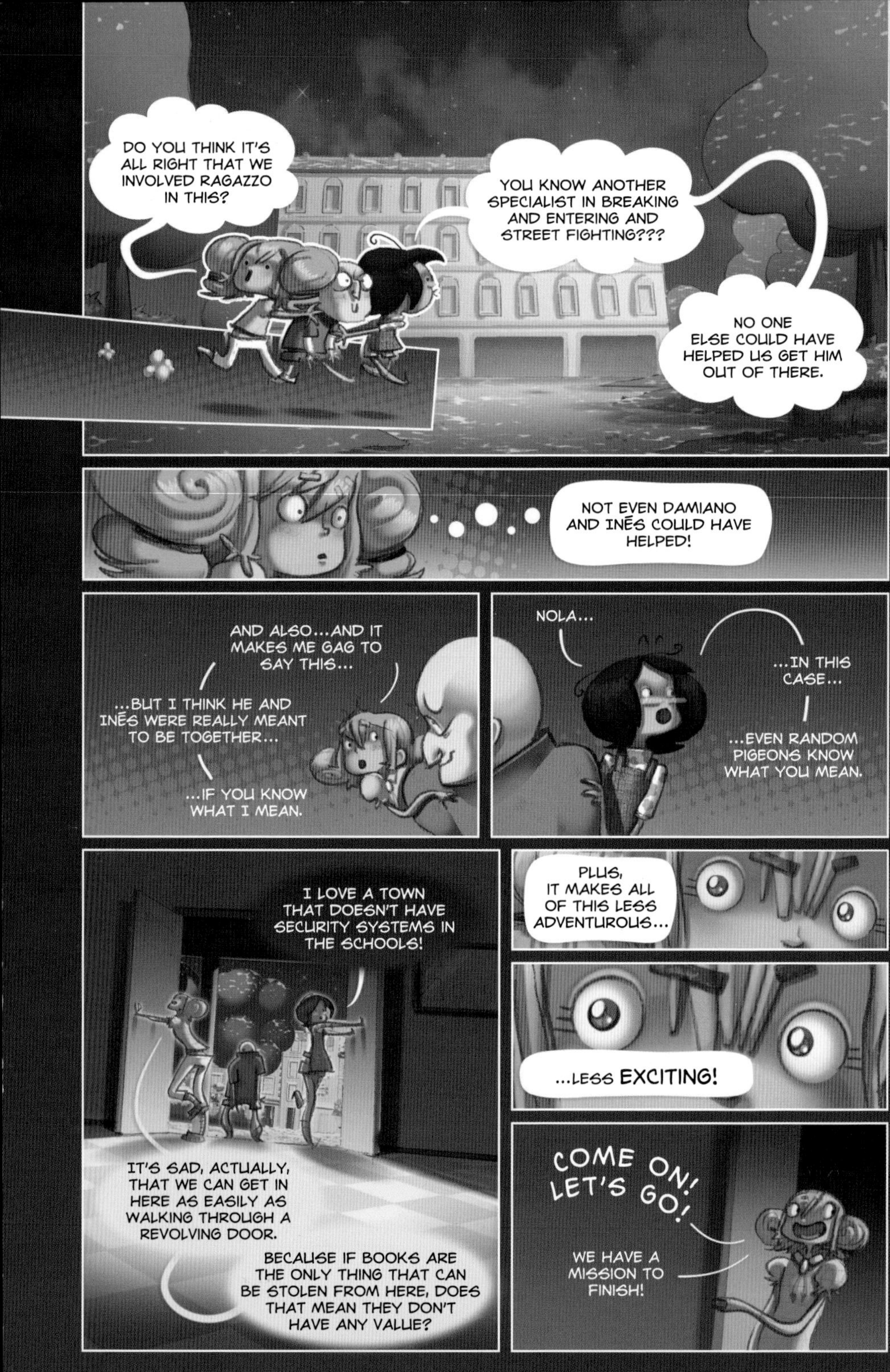
DO YOU THINK IT'S ALL RIGHT THAT WE INVOLVED RAGAZZO IN THIS?
YOU KNOW ANOTHER SPECIALIST IN BREAKING AND ENTERING AND STREET FIGHTING???
NO ONE ELSE COULD HAVE HELPED US GET HIM OUT OF THERE.
NOT EVEN DAMIANO AND INÉS COULD HAVE HELPED!
AND ALSO...AND IT MAKES ME GAG TO SAY THIS...
...BUT I THINK HE AND INÉS WERE REALLY MEANT TO BE TOGETHER...
...IF YOU KNOW WHAT I MEAN.
NOLA...
...IN THIS CASE...
...EVEN RANDOM PIGEONS KNOW WHAT YOU MEAN.
I LOVE A TOWN THAT DOESN'T HAVE SECURITY SYSTEMS IN THE SCHOOLS!
IT'S SAD, ACTUALLY, THAT WE CAN GET IN HERE AS EASILY AS WALKING THROUGH A REVOLVING DOOR.
BECAUSE IF BOOKS ARE THE ONLY THING THAT CAN BE STOLEN FROM HERE, DOES THAT MEAN THEY DON'T HAVE ANY VALUE?
PLUS, IT MAKES ALL OF THIS LESS ADVENTUROUS...
...LESS EXCITING!
COME ON! LET'S GO!
WE HAVE A MISSION TO FINISH!

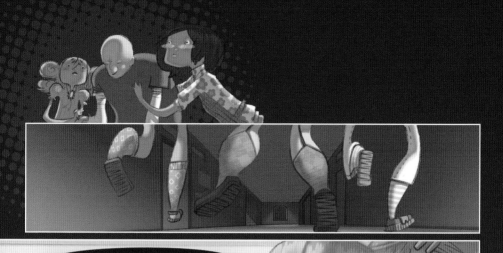

OoOOHHH!

HOW THOUGHTFUL OF YOU TO BRING US OUR OLD FRIEND.

SINCE I'VE BEEN PINING TO SEE HIM AGAIN.

YOU!

WHEN SHE SAYS "YOU," D'YOU THINK...

...SHE MEANS US TOO??

OR JUST THE BOSS LADY???

THE BOSS!

THE BOSS LADY!

THE BOSS!

SHUT UP!!!

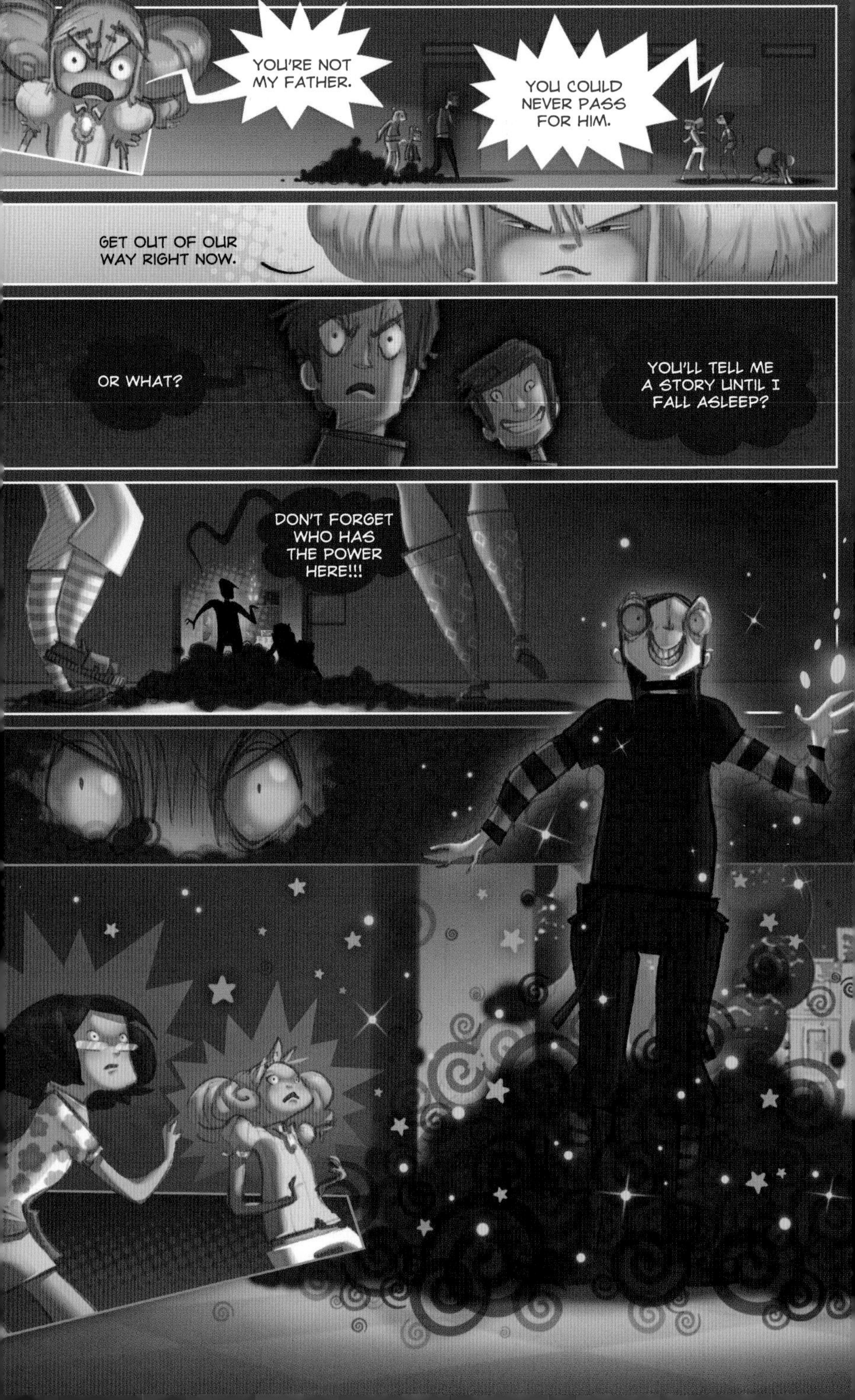
YOU'RE NOT MY FATHER.
YOU COULD NEVER PASS FOR HIM.
GET OUT OF OUR WAY RIGHT NOW.
OR WHAT?
YOU'LL TELL ME A STORY UNTIL I FALL ASLEEP?
DON'T FORGET WHO HAS THE POWER HERE!!!

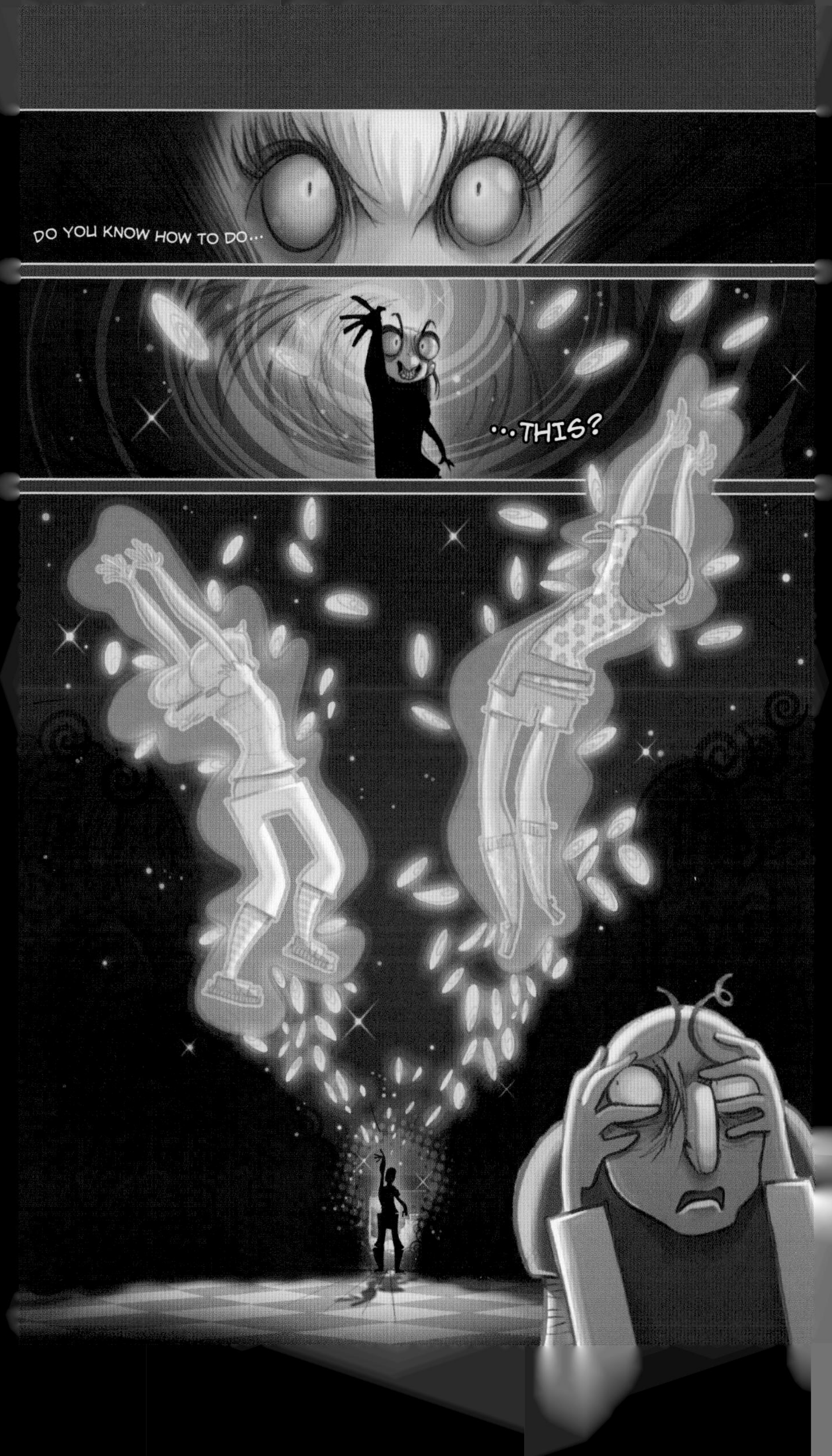
DO YOU KNOW HOW TO DO...
...THIS?

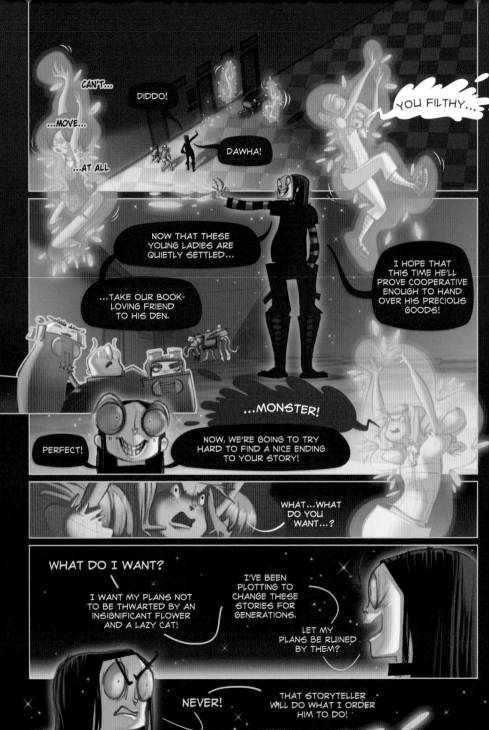

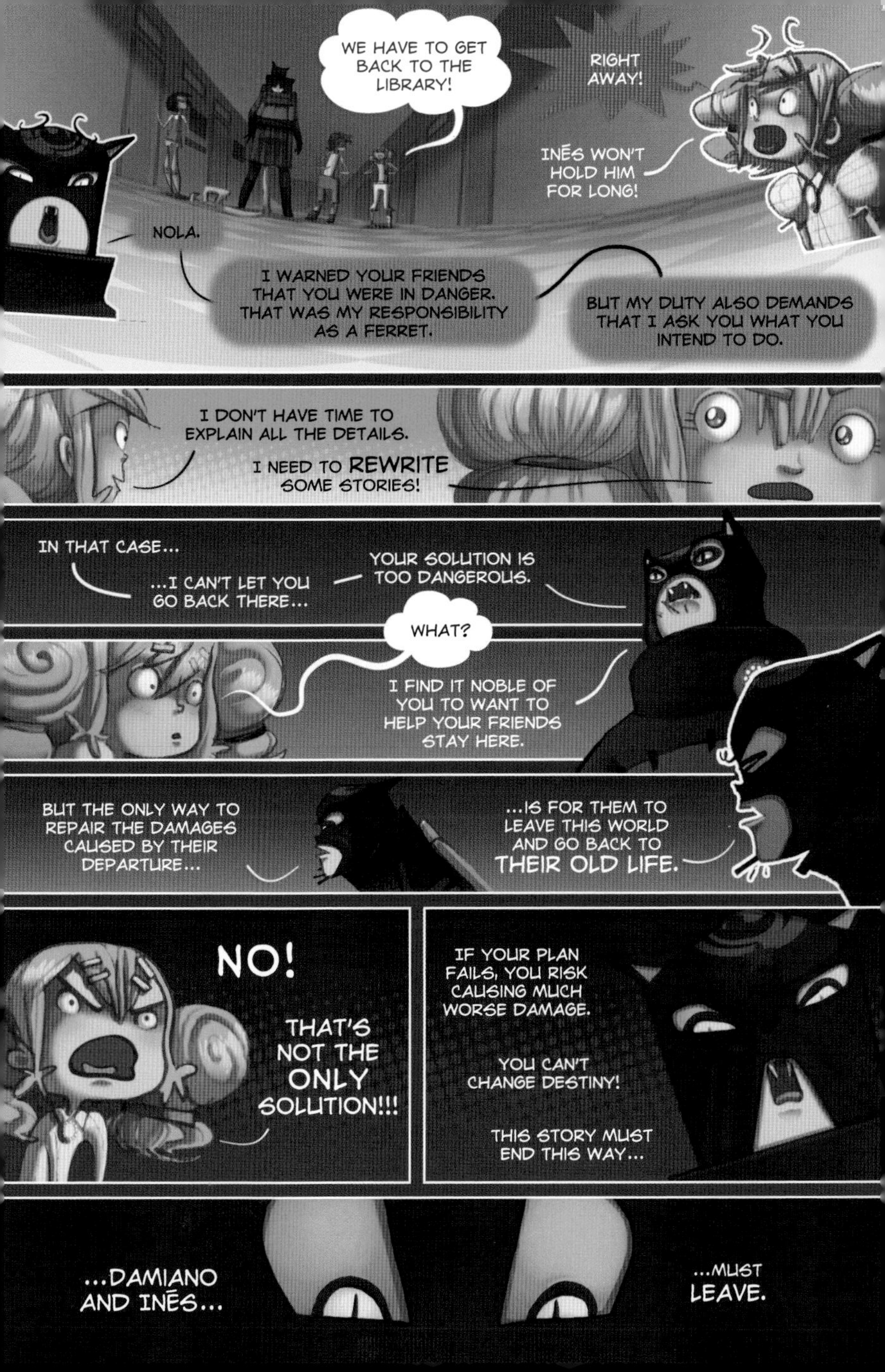

WE HAVE TO GET BACK TO THE LIBRARY!
RIGHT AWAY!
INÉS WON'T HOLD HIM FOR LONG!
NOLA.
I WARNED YOUR FRIENDS THAT YOU WERE IN DANGER. THAT WAS MY RESPONSIBILITY AS A FERRET.
BUT MY DUTY ALSO DEMANDS THAT I ASK YOU WHAT YOU INTEND TO DO.
I DON'T HAVE TIME TO EXPLAIN ALL THE DETAILS.
I NEED TO REWRITE SOME STORIES!
IN THAT CASE...
...I CAN'T LET YOU GO BACK THERE...
YOUR SOLUTION IS TOO DANGEROUS.
WHAT?
I FIND IT NOBLE OF YOU TO WANT TO HELP YOUR FRIENDS STAY HERE.
BUT THE ONLY WAY TO REPAIR THE DAMAGES CAUSED BY THEIR DEPARTURE...
...IS FOR THEM TO LEAVE THIS WORLD AND GO BACK TO THEIR OLD LIFE.
NO!
THAT'S NOT THE ONLY SOLUTION!!!
IF YOUR PLAN FAILS, YOU RISK CAUSING MUCH WORSE DAMAGE.
YOU CAN'T CHANGE DESTINY!
THIS STORY MUST END THIS WAY...
...DAMIANO AND INÉS...
...MUST LEAVE.

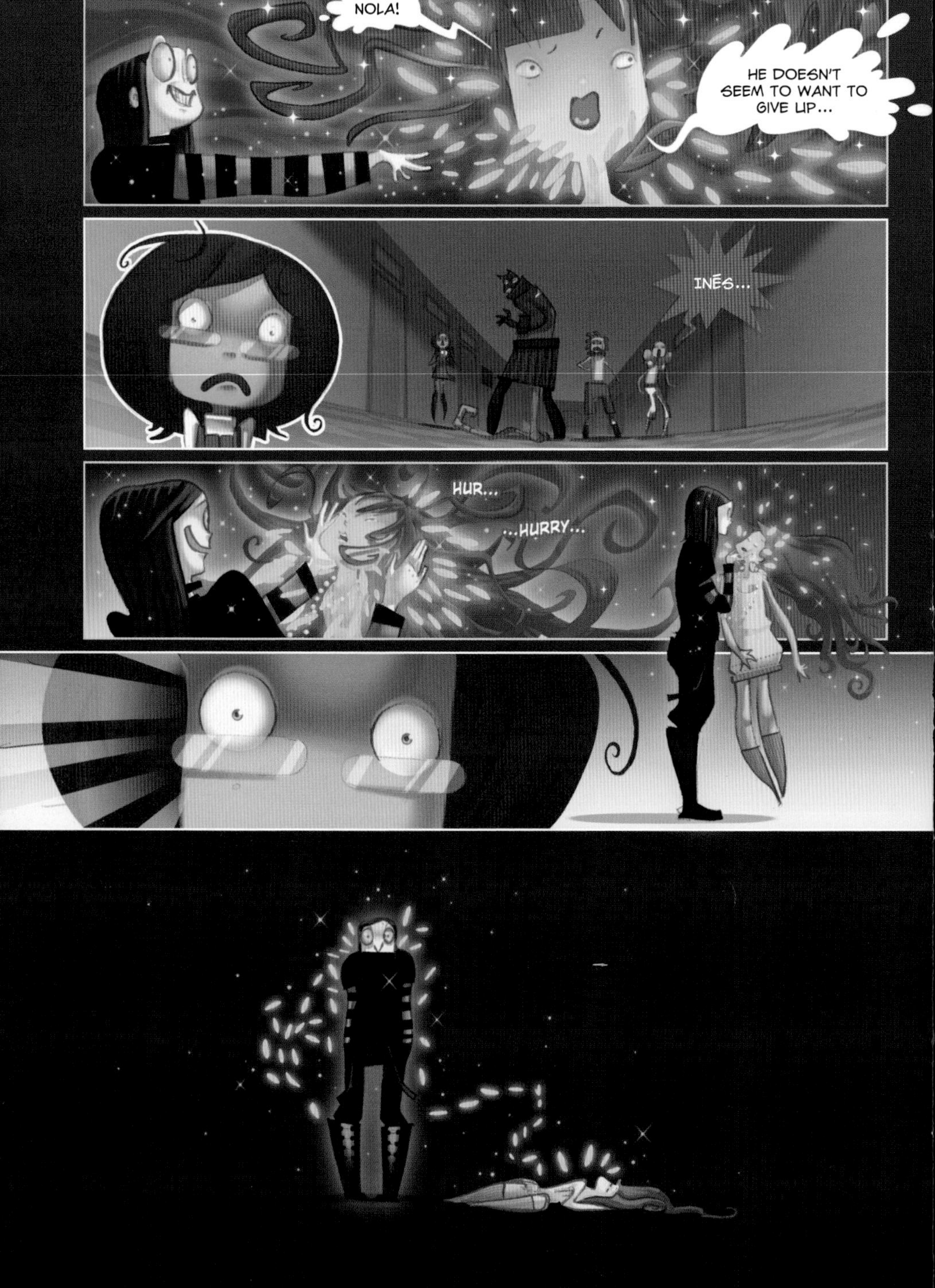
NOLA!
HE DOESN'T SEEM TO WANT TO GIVE UP...
INÉS...
HUR...
...HURRY...

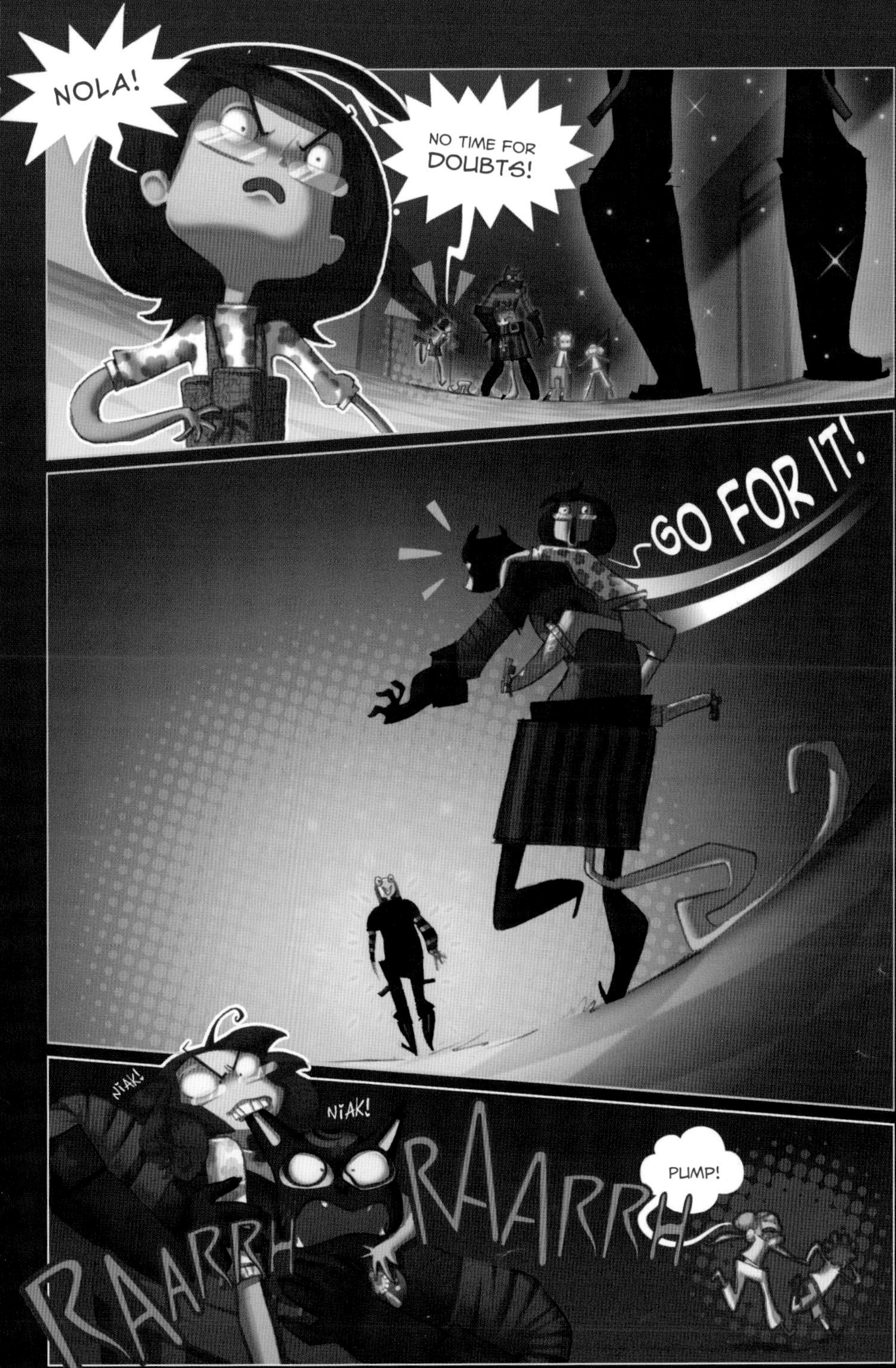
NOLA!
NO TIME FOR DOUBTS!
GO FOR IT!
NIAK!
NIAK!
RAARRH
RAARRH
PUMP!

MY PLAN ENDS HERE...
I DON'T KNOW HOW TO REWRITE THE STORIES!
I WAS HOPING HE WOULD TELL US HOW.
TELL US WHERE THE BOOK IS!!!

122

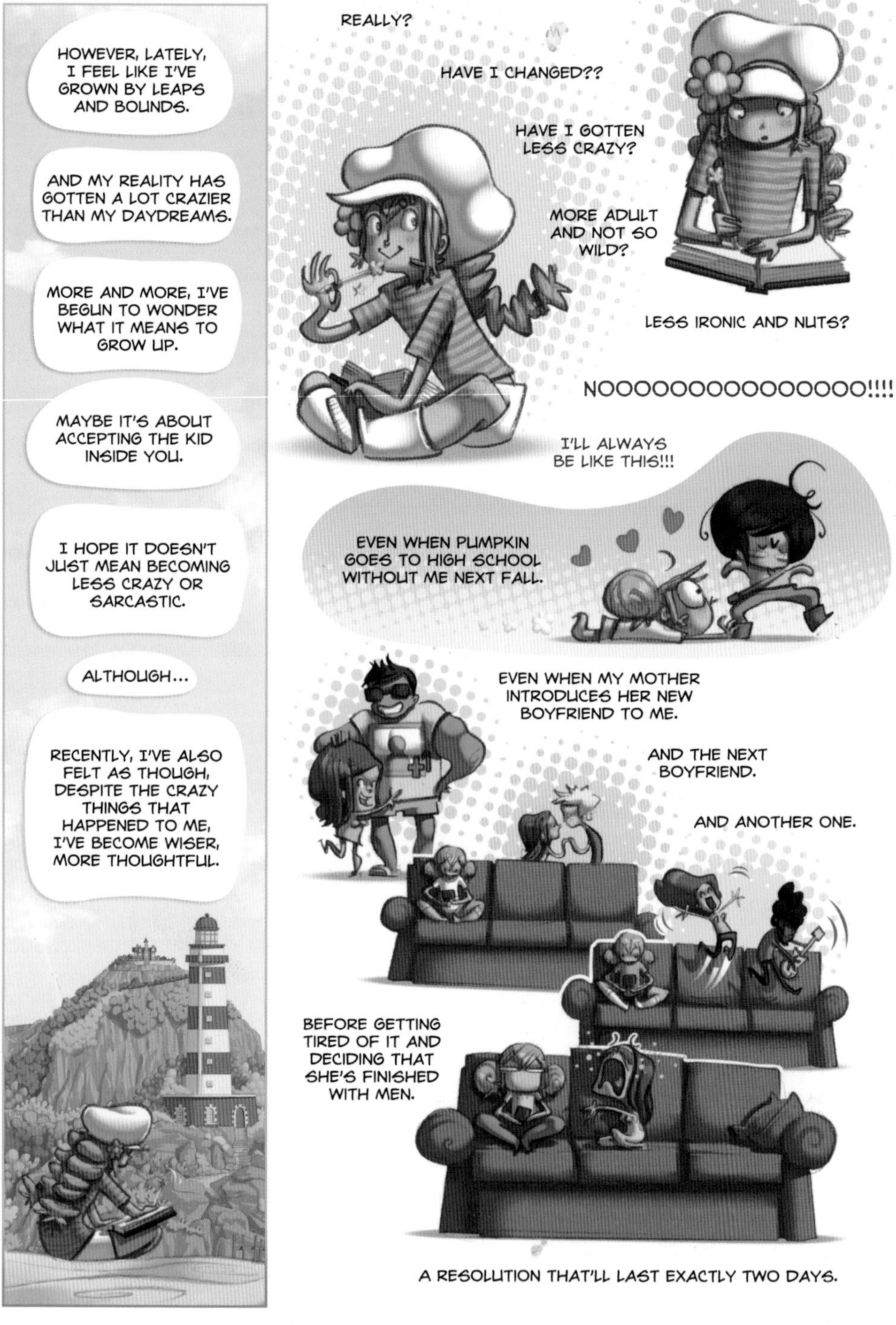
HOWEVER, LATELY, I FEEL LIKE I'VE GROWN BY LEAPS AND BOUNDS.
AND MY REALITY HAS GOTTEN A LOT CRAZIER THAN MY DAYDREAMS.
MORE AND MORE, I'VE BEGUN TO WONDER WHAT IT MEANS TO GROW UP.
MAYBE IT'S ABOUT ACCEPTING THE KID INSIDE YOU.
I HOPE IT DOESN'T JUST MEAN BECOMING LESS CRAZY OR SARCASTIC.
ALTHOUGH...
RECENTLY, I'VE ALSO FELT AS THOUGH, DESPITE THE CRAZY THINGS THAT HAPPENED TO ME, I'VE BECOME WISER, MORE THOUGHTFUL.
REALLY?
HAVE I CHANGED??
HAVE I GOTTEN LESS CRAZY?
MORE ADULT AND NOT SO WILD?
LESS IRONIC AND NUTS?
NOOOOOOOOOOOOOOO!!!!
I'LL ALWAYS BE LIKE THIS!!!
EVEN WHEN PUMPKIN GOES TO HIGH SCHOOL WITHOUT ME NEXT FALL.
EVEN WHEN MY MOTHER INTRODUCES HER NEW BOYFRIEND TO ME.
AND THE NEXT BOYFRIEND.
AND ANOTHER ONE.
BEFORE GETTING TIRED OF IT AND DECIDING THAT SHE'S FINISHED WITH MEN.
A RESOLUTION THAT'LL LAST EXACTLY TWO DAYS.

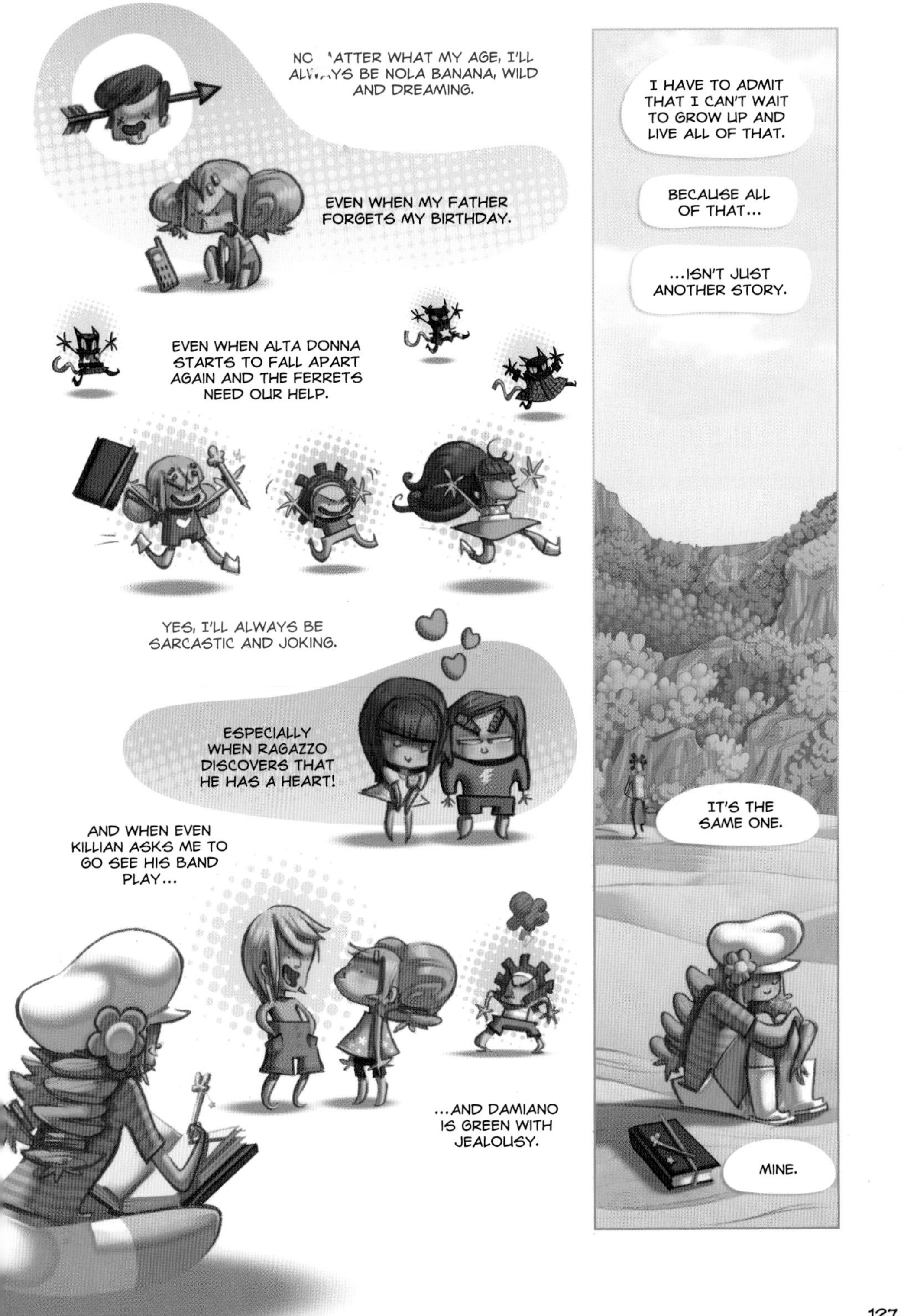
NO MATTER WHAT MY AGE, I'LL ALWAYS BE NOLA BANANA, WILD AND DREAMING.
EVEN WHEN MY FATHER FORGETS MY BIRTHDAY.
EVEN WHEN ALTA DONNA STARTS TO FALL APART AGAIN AND THE FERRETS NEED OUR HELP.
YES, I'LL ALWAYS BE SARCASTIC AND JOKING.
ESPECIALLY WHEN RAGAZZO DISCOVERS THAT HE HAS A HEART!
AND WHEN EVEN KILLIAN ASKS ME TO GO SEE HIS BAND PLAY...
...AND DAMIANO IS GREEN WITH JEALOUSY.
I HAVE TO ADMIT THAT I CAN'T WAIT TO GROW UP AND LIVE ALL OF THAT.
BECAUSE ALL OF THAT...
...ISN'T JUST ANOTHER STORY.
IT'S THE SAME ONE.
MINE.